The One and Only

WITHDRAWN

A Maryellen Classic
Volume 1

by Valerie Tripp

★ American Girl®

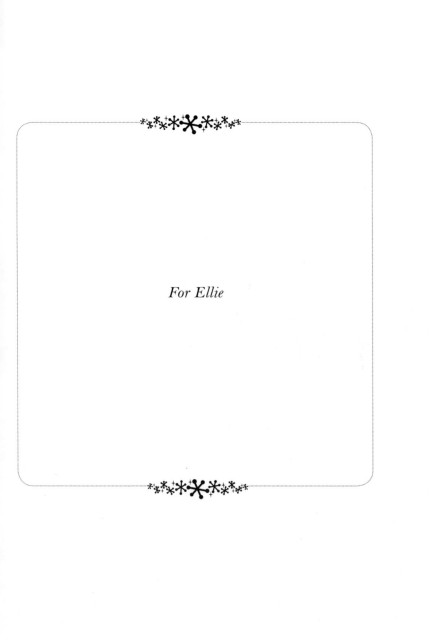

For Ellie

Beforever™

The adventurous characters you'll meet in
the BeForever books will spark your curiosity
about the past, inspire you to find your voice
in the present, and excite you about your future.
You'll make friends with these girls as you share
their fun and their challenges. Like you, they are
bright and brave, imaginative and energetic,
creative and kind. Just as you are, they are
discovering what really matters: Helping others.
Being a true friend. Protecting the earth.
Standing up for what's right. Read their stories,
explore their worlds, join their adventures.
Your friendship with them will BeForever.

✷ TABLE *of* CONTENTS ✷

The Room Switcheroo

aryellen Larkin liked to make up episodes of her favorite TV shows and imagine herself in them. This morning, for example, as Maryellen was walking down the hot, sunny sidewalk with her dog, Scooter, to mail a letter to her grandparents, she was pretending that she was in an episode of the exciting Western *The Lone Ranger*. Her only companion was her trusty horse, Thunderbolt. (That was Scooter's part.) Maryellen leaned forward as if she were battling her way through a blinding blizzard. If she didn't deliver the medicine in her hand, hundreds of people would die.

Maryellen never gave herself superpowers in any of her imagined shows. She didn't fly or do magic or become invisible or anything. She looked the way she really looked, except maybe a little taller and with better clothes. The main difference was that in her TV shows, everyone paid attention to her. They listened to her great ideas, they followed her advice, and—*ta-da!*—everything turned out just right.

Maryellen ceremoniously put her letter in the mailbox, imagining that she was handing medicine to a kindly old doctor in the snowy town in the Old West. "Thank you, Miss Larkin, ma'am," the imaginary doctor said. "We desperately needed this. You have saved hundreds of lives today."

Maryellen smiled modestly and shrugged as if to say, "It was nothing." Then she turned to go. "Come on, Thunderbolt," she said to Scooter. "Our work is done."

Scooter, a stout and elderly dachshund, had *just* flopped down and made himself comfortable in the shade of the mailbox. But Maryellen whispered, "Come on, Scooter. Get up, old boy." So Scooter rose with a good-natured sigh and waddled behind Maryellen, who pretended to trudge through drifts of snow as grateful townspeople called after her, "Thank you, Miss Larkin! You're our hero!"

"Hey, Ellie," said a real voice, calling her by her nickname. The voice belonged to her friend Davy

Fenstermacher, who lived next door in a house that looked exactly like the Larkins' house. Maryellen and Davy had been friends forever.

"Howdy, pardner," Maryellen drawled.

"I'll race you to the swing!" said Davy. "On your mark, get set, *go*!"

Maryellen and Davy ran to the Larkins' backyard, with Scooter loping along behind them. Maryellen got to the swing first, jumped on, and began to pump. "I win!" she called down to Davy. "You be the Lone Ranger, stuck in quicksand, and I'll jump down and rescue you."

"Okay," said Davy agreeably. Of course, they both knew that cowboys didn't usually jump off swings. But the swing that Mr. Larkin had hung in the backyard was so much fun that they used it in lots of the TV shows they made up.

Maryellen swung high and then jumped off. "Ya*hoo*!" she hollered, swooping through the August air. She landed on the grass with a soft thud. "Come on, Thunderbolt!" she called to Scooter. "We've got to save the Lone Ranger!"

Scooter, asleep in the shade, snored.

"Better wake him up first, Ellie," said Davy.

But before Maryellen could rouse Scooter, her six-year-old sister, Beverly, came clomping out of the house in an old pair of Mrs. Larkin's high heels. Beverly wore one of Dad's baseball caps turned inside out so that it looked like a crown. She also wore three pop-bead necklaces and two pop-bead bracelets, one on each arm. Right behind Beverly came Tom and Mikey, Maryellen's younger brothers. They were four and not-quite-two years old.

"What are you doing?" Beverly asked.

"Nothing," said Maryellen, wishing that Beverly and the boys would go back inside, but knowing that they wouldn't. Maryellen, Beverly, Tom, and Mikey shared a bedroom, and even though the little kids were cute and sweet and goofy, they drove Maryellen crazy, especially the boys. One time, while she was at school, the boys got into her *I Love Lucy* paper dolls and she found Lucy's clothes scattered all over the floor like confetti and Lucy folded up in one of Tom's toy trucks. Lucy had never been able to hold her head up again. Now that it was summer, Beverly, Tom, and Mikey stuck to her like glue, twenty-four hours a day. They couldn't bear to be left out of anything fun that she might be doing.

Sure enough, Beverly said, "I want to play with you and Davy!"

"Me too!" said Tom.

"Me!" said Mikey.

Davy shot Maryellen a sympathetic look. He had years of experience dealing with Beverly, Tom, and Mikey.

Thinking quickly, Maryellen suggested to Davy, "What if the little kids are in the quicksand, too, and I rescue all of you?"

"Good idea," said Davy.

"Pretend I'm a queen that you're rescuing," said Beverly.

"Oh, brother," Maryellen muttered. That was another problem with Beverly. She liked to pretend, but she always pretended the same thing: that she was a queen. Dad called her Queen Beverly. "I don't think they had queens in the Wild West," Maryellen said. "I've never seen one on a TV show, anyway. Have you, Davy?"

"Nope," said Davy firmly.

Maryellen smiled. Good old Davy always backed her up. She said to Beverly, clinching the point, "And Davy and I have watched almost every TV show there ever was."

Queen Beverly looked stubborn. Maryellen was just about to give in to Her Majesty when their mother called out the back door, "Ellie, honey, come in for a minute. I need you."

"Okay," called Maryellen, feeling pleased. Mom needed *her*!

Maryellen's pride wilted just a bit when Mom added, "Beverly, Tom, and Mikey, you come, too." She wished Mom wouldn't always lump her together with Beverly, Tom, and Mikey as if they were one big bumpy creature with four heads, eight arms, and eight legs. Mom certainly treated Maryellen's older sisters, Joan and Carolyn, as separate, serious people.

I'm tired of being one of the "little kids," grumped Maryellen to herself, for the millionth time. *I guess I'm stuck with Beverly, but I'm much too grown-up to share a room with Tom and Mikey. Somehow, I have to convince Mom that I should share a bedroom with Joan and Carolyn so that she'll think of me as one of the "big girls" and take me—and my ideas—more seriously.*

"Come on, kids," said Mom. She scooped Mikey up onto her hip and held out her free hand to Tom. Beverly clomped along as quickly as she could in her high heels. Scooter rose stiffly and followed her.

"What do you need us for, Mom?" asked Maryellen.

"Just a quick family meeting," said Mom.

"Oh," said Maryellen without enthusiasm. She knew from experience that it was hard to get a word in edgewise during family meetings. They were not at all like one of her pretend TV shows where she was the hero and everyone hung on her every word. Maryellen sighed and said to Davy, "See you later, alligator."

"In a while, crocodile," said Davy. "I'll wait here."

Maryellen walked into the kitchen and slid onto the bench in the breakfast nook next to Joan, her eldest sister. Joan, who was seventeen and therefore nearly all grown-up, looked sideways at Maryellen's grass-stained shorts and inched away, closer to Carolyn. It was crowded on the bench, but Maryellen wanted Mom to see her next to Joan and Carolyn, on their side of the table, so that Mom would think of the three of them as a group.

Maryellen could tell that this family meeting

would be like all the others: frustrating. The kitchen was already noisy. Dad had left on a three-day business trip earlier that morning, but Mom and Carolyn, Maryellen's next-oldest sister, were talking a mile a minute. Tom was wailing like a siren as he rode his toy fire truck around the kitchen. Mikey was yodeling and banging a spoon on the tray connected to his high chair. Mrs. Larkin took Mikey's spoon away from him and gave him a piece of toast, which was quieter to bang, and then said, "Kids!"

Everyone quieted down.

"I have an important announcement," said Mrs. Larkin. "My friends Betty and Florence are coming to spend the night."

"Who're Fletty and Borence?" asked Beverly.

"*B*etty and *Fl*orence," said Mrs. Larkin. "You kids have never met them. We worked together at the factory. They live in New York City now. We're going to a reunion luncheon at the factory tomorrow." Maryellen knew that Mom was referring to the aircraft factory where she had worked during World War Two.

"I'm glad Betty and Florence are coming," said Maryellen. Her mind sped ahead. Lots of TV quiz shows were filmed in New York City. Maybe Mom's friends could get her a spot on one of them! She'd be the youngest contestant *ever*—

Joan interrupted Maryellen's daydream with a practical question. "Where will Betty and Florence sleep?" she asked Mom.

Maryellen's mind sped ahead again. This could be the moment she had been waiting for all summer! "I have an idea," she announced.

But Mom didn't hear Maryellen. No one did. Mom was saying, "I guess they'll have to sleep on the sofa bed in the living room, though that doesn't seem very welcoming."

"I've got an idea," Maryellen said again. She popped up from her place at the table and went over and tugged on her mother's sleeve. "Listen!"

But Mrs. Larkin just patted Maryellen's hand and gave her a wink and a smile while everyone kept talking as much and as loudly as ever.

Maryellen grabbed Mikey's spoon and pounded it on the table the way she'd seen judges pound gavels in TV courtroom drama shows. "HEY!" she shouted as loud as she could. "Order in the court!"

Mom winced and held her hands over her ears. "Ellie, sweetie pie, settle down," she scolded gently. "Please don't shout and bang the table like Mikey. It's childish."

"Sorry, Mom," said Maryellen, red in the face. The last thing she wanted was for Mom to think that she was childish. "But listen—I have a great idea!"

"Tell us," said Mom. "You have our attention."

"Please don't suggest that Mom's friends should sleep in hammocks swinging from trees," Joan teased. "Not everyone enjoys pretending to be Tarzan, King of the Apes, like you and Davy were just now."

"We *weren't* being Tarzan," Maryellen said, "and I *wasn't* going to suggest hammocks, though I bet they'd be fun to sleep in. But actually, I think Mom's guests should sleep in *your* room."

"*My* room?" said Joan. "That's impossible! Carolyn and I hardly fit in there together as it is."

"We're squooshed!" Carolyn agreed. Carolyn was fourteen, and easygoing. She and Joan shared a set of bunk beds in a tiny bedroom.

"I have it all figured out," said Maryellen. "Joan, you and Carolyn will give your room to Betty and

Florence. You'll sleep in the big bedroom with Beverly and me, in Tom and Mikey's bunk beds, and the boys will sleep in Mom and Dad's room." Maryellen smiled at Tom. "You *like* sleeping on the floor, don't you?"

"Yes!" said Tom. He looked happy. But then, Tom just about always looked happy. With spiky yellow hair sticking straight out all over his head, he looked like a cheerful dandelion.

Joan frowned. She started to say, "I don't—"

But Mom interrupted, "Why, Maryellen Larkin! I do believe you've hit upon a solution to our problem."

Maryellen beamed, although she wished that Mom hadn't sounded quite so surprised that she had had a good idea. Flushed with her success, she rattled on eagerly. "After Betty and Florence leave," she said, "Tom and Mikey can move into the little room, and the big room will be the All Girls Room." Maryellen was sure that sharing a room with Joan and Carolyn would change everything for her, and change the way everyone thought of her and treated her, too. They'd see that she was mature. After all, she was nearly ten. She was going to be in the fourth grade!

Everyone started to talk at once again.

"We can decorate the All Girls Room with pictures of TV stars," said Maryellen.

"What?" said Joan.

"TV stars!" said Carolyn.

"Goodie!" said Beverly.

"But, but," Joan sputtered, "that means *four* of us will share *one* closet and—"

"Whoa!" said Mrs. Larkin, holding up both hands. "Hold it, everyone." She turned to Maryellen and said, "Ellie, dear, you're getting carried away, as usual. We'll give Betty and Florence the little room tonight. But let's do one thing at a time, okay?"

"Sure, Mom," said Maryellen.

"All right then," said Mrs. Larkin. "Meeting adjourned."

Mom lifted Mikey out of his high chair, and he toddled behind Beverly and Tom to go watch cartoons on TV. But as Maryellen, Carolyn, and Mom started to leave, Joan stopped them.

"Just for the record," said Joan, "I'm not crazy about this whole room switcheroo."

"Why not?" asked Maryellen.

"Scooter, for starters," said Joan. "I don't want to

share a room with him. You let him sleep on your bed, for heaven's sake, and he has bad breath and he drools and he sheds and he *snores*."

Maryellen wished Dad were home. He always defended Scooter. Everyone glanced over at Scooter now. Scooter managed to snore, drool, scratch himself, and send a flurry of hair into the air all at the same time. Maryellen sighed. She had to admit that Joan had a point.

"Maybe Scooter can sleep in the living room?" Carolyn suggested gently.

Maryellen felt disloyal to Scooter, but she said, "I guess so."

"Scooter's not the only problem," said Joan.

"*Now* what?" said Maryellen, rolling her eyes.

"You," said Joan. "You're sloppy."

Maryellen could see that her sweaty hair and grimy hands were a sharp contrast to Joan's crisp, clean appearance. "Well, maybe I'm a little messy right *now*," she said honestly. She smoothed her rumpled T-shirt, which was a faded and stained hand-me-down from Carolyn. "I was playing outdoors."

"I know," said Joan. "You were goofing around with

Davy like a wild tomboy, as usual. *That'll* have to stop soon anyway, because you can't be friends with a boy in fourth grade."

Maryellen frowned. "Why not?"

"It just doesn't work. You wait and see," Joan went on. "But it's not only your appearance that's grubby. Your bed, your drawers, your closet—*all* your things are messy. Last night, you flooded the bathroom, and before that, you stepped in the popcorn bowl and overturned it. Face it, Ellie—you create a disaster area wherever you go."

"Hey!" said Carolyn, sticking up for Maryellen. "Just because Ellie's not persnickety like you doesn't mean she's a hopeless mess."

"Right!" said Maryellen indignantly. "And I don't create disasters. Do I, Mom?"

"Well," said Mrs. Larkin, "I think what Joan means is that you're not very tidy or organized, honey."

"See?" said Joan. "I don't think it's fair that I should have to share a room with such a messy little kid."

"A messy little kid?" Maryellen repeated, horrified. Granted, she was not a finicky fussbudget like Joan. But a *messy little kid*? One who was childish, wild, untidy, tomboyish, disorganized, and grubby? A messy little kid who created disasters wherever she went? Was that how Joan and—Maryellen gulped—*Mom* thought of her?

"Let's say this," said Mrs. Larkin. "We'll give the All Girls Room a try tonight. Sharing a room with your big sisters will be a test for you, Ellie. If you show that you can be tidy and responsible, we'll consider making the All Girls Room permanent. Do we have a deal, ladies?"

"I suppose so," said Joan with a shrug.

"It's fine with me," said Carolyn.

"Yes," said Maryellen. She understood that if she failed this test, she'd lose her chance for the All Girls Room. But there was something even more important than that at stake. If she failed the test, she'd lose her chance to improve Mom's opinion of her.

"That's settled, then," said Mom. "Joan and Carolyn, come with me and I'll give you fresh bedsheets. And you'd better move your pajamas and whatever else you'll need for tonight into Ellie's room. Ellie, if I were you, I'd start a Cleanup Campaign right away."

"I will, Mom," said Maryellen.

While the others headed to the linen closet, Maryellen dashed outside to speak to Davy.

"Looks like I'll be inside for a while," she said. "I've got to clean up my room."

"How come?" asked Davy. He was sitting on the swing, spinning to make himself dizzy.

Maryellen explained about the room switcheroo. "Joan didn't want to do it," she said, "because she thinks I'm messy. Mom said that she had to, but that it'll be a test for me."

"A test of what?" asked Davy.

"Neatness, mostly," Maryellen said, "and being careful of what I do."

Davy grinned. "Or what you *don't* do," he said. "Just *don't* make a mess."

"Right!" said Maryellen, cheered up by Davy as usual. "That'll be easy!"

Another Great Idea

CHAPTER TWO

U sually, when Mom asked Maryellen to clean up her room, she gave it a lick and a wish, shoving her clothes into drawers, tossing her shoes into the closet, and yanking the bed covers up. But now, Maryellen folded her clothes neatly, lined up her shoes in the closet, and pulled her covers taut, so that not one lump or wrinkle could be seen. Maryellen liked to sketch, so she made a little drawing of Joan and Carolyn, wrote "Welcome!" on it, and taped it to the mirror. Then she dusted the top of the bureau, in case Joan and Carolyn wanted to put their brushes and combs there.

"Look, Mom," she said. "*Ta-da!* I made everything tidy and beautiful."

Mrs. Larkin gave Maryellen's work a quick glance. "Good," she said. She sounded a little out of breath because she was standing on the lower bunk bed tucking a sheet under the mattress of the upper bunk.

Mom didn't seem overly impressed by her efforts, so Maryellen looked around to see what else she could do. She collected Tom's trucks and Mikey's blocks in a box and slid the box under the bed. Then she took some shirts off two hooks on the closet door so that Joan and Carolyn could hang their pajamas on the hooks.

As Maryellen was hanging the shirts on hangers in the closet, Joan and Carolyn appeared, their arms full. Maryellen was delighted to see that in addition to her pajamas, Joan was bringing her tennis dress, bobby pins, cold cream, and several books and magazines. Carolyn was bringing some clothes, some rock 'n' roll records, and her portable record player.

Now that's more like it! thought Maryellen. *Instead of babyish toy trucks and blocks, the All Girls Room will be full of grown-up things like books, rock 'n' roll records, and movie-star magazines.*

"You need all that for *one* night?" asked Mom, shaking her head at Joan and Carolyn.

"Not all of it is for me," said Carolyn. "I thought while I was at it, I might as well move these dresses

I've outgrown into Ellie's closet." Carolyn showed
Maryellen a plaid dress. "I wore this dress to the first
day of fourth grade," she said, "so I thought you'd like
to, too."

"Uh, thanks," said Maryellen, polite but not
thrilled.

"Hey," said Joan, "I remember that dress. I wore it
in fourth grade, too. I used to think it was so cute."

When Joan and Carolyn left, Maryellen held the
plaid dress up in front of herself as she looked in the
mirror. She sighed. "Mom," she said, "don't you think
this hand-me-down dress is sort of old and worn-out?"

"Umph," said Mom. She was holding a pillow
under her chin as she slipped a fresh pillowcase onto it.

"I sure would love a brand-new outfit to wear for
the first day of fourth grade," said Maryellen. She got
carried away, imagining herself in a chic, fashionable,
grown-up-looking outfit like the ones girls wore on
TV shows. Oh boy! *Everyone* would be impressed!
The perfect back-to-school dress would guarantee
the perfect start to school and a perfect year in fourth
grade. She said eagerly, "Mom, you and I should go
shopping and—"

"Maryellen!" Mrs. Larkin interrupted in a no-nonsense voice. "Carolyn's plaid dress is perfectly fine for your first day of school. You don't need anything new, except maybe some socks and underwear. But right now, I can't even *think* about a shopping trip. I've got my hands full getting ready for Betty and Florence. Now come and help me gather up these sheets for the laundry."

"Okay, Mom," said Maryellen. She was disappointed, but even new underwear was better than nothing. And she knew better than to press her luck. Mom sounded unusually harried. As one of six children, Maryellen had long ago learned the sad but true lesson that parents had only a certain amount of patience and energy and attention to give, and you couldn't use more than your share or your parents got mad. So she just quietly helped Mom with the sheets. She'd save the shopping conversation for later.

✳

After lunch, Mrs. Larkin said, "Kids, I've got to scrub the kitchen floor. I need you out of my hair and out of the house for a while. So put on your swimsuits

and go to the beach." She turned to Davy, who had
come over for lunch, and said, "Davy, ask your mom if
you may go, too, if you like."

The girls hurried off to put on their swimsuits. The
Larkins lived in Daytona Beach, Florida, just a few
blocks from the ocean. Maryellen felt lucky that on hot
days like this one, she could go to the beach to swim
and cool off.

Maryellen was ready in a flash, so she went back to
the kitchen, where Mom was helping Mikey put on his
bathing trunks. Maryellen saw an old photo that she'd
never seen before on the kitchen table. The photo was
of Mom and two smiling ladies standing in front of a
factory. Maryellen immediately figured out that the
two ladies were Betty and Florence. "Hey, Mom," she
asked as she looked at the photo, "what did you and
Betty and Florence do at the factory?"

"Well, they worked on the assembly line, and I was
the line manager," said Mrs. Larkin.

"The manager?" repeated Maryellen. "You mean
you were the boss of the whole assembly line?"

"I sure was," said Mom, tying Mikey's shoelaces.

Maryellen was stunned. She had never realized that

Mom had had such an important job! And now Mom just stayed home and made life organized and smooth and pleasant for their family. "What do Betty and Florence do now?" Maryellen asked.

"They're executive secretaries at an airline company in New York," said Mom.

"Oh," said Maryellen. Mom's friends' jobs sounded swank and fancy. She asked, "Are you sorry you're not working now, Mom?"

"Ellie, my dear," said Mom in a jokey way as she pulled a T-shirt down over Mikey's head, "managing you kids is harder work than managing the assembly line was."

"Be serious, Mom," said Maryellen.

"I am!" said Mom. "I'm seriously proud of our family, and proud of doing a good job of running our house. This is my job right now, and I like it. But nothing is forever. When Mikey is in school all day, maybe I'll go back to work."

"But what work would you do?" asked Carolyn, who had wandered into the kitchen with Beverly.

"I don't know," said Mrs. Larkin. She looped a wisp of hair behind her ear. "I might work in an office, or be a saleslady in a store, or—"

"Or a movie star!" Beverly piped up.

Mrs. Larkin laughed. "I don't think I'll be a movie star," she said, "though it would be nice to look glamorous, and to smell like perfume instead of peanut butter for a change."

By now, everyone was ready to go. Mom handed some beach towels to Joan and said, "Okay, troops! Off you go to the beach. Be back by two, no later. Joan, keep an eye on the little ones. Vamoose!"

"Okay, Mom," everyone said. "Bye!"

Davy joined the parade of Larkins walking to the beach, falling into step with Scooter and Maryellen. "What's up, Doc?" Davy asked, pretending to be Bugs Bunny.

"I'm thinking about Mom," said Maryellen, "and what her life was like when she had a job during the war. Guess what? It turns out that Mom was important! She was a line boss at the factory."

"Wow!" said Davy. "Why'd she quit?"

"Lots of women quit working after the war," said Carolyn, "so the returning soldiers could have jobs."

"Mom shouldn't have quit. She was famous,"

Beverly sighed, "like a movie star."

"Well, she wasn't exactly a movie star, but she was the star of the factory back when Betty and Florence worked with her," said Maryellen. "And now Mom's life is about as exciting and glamorous as . . . as . . ."

"Scooter's," Davy finished for her.

"Yes," sighed Maryellen. Her heart swelled with love and sympathy for Mom. Probably Mom felt sort of taken for granted. Maryellen knew how *that* felt. Surely Mom missed standing out and being admired, as she had been when she was an important boss at the factory. Maryellen made up her mind right then: *I'm going to think of a way for Mom to impress her friends.* Her next thought made her so excited, her heart skipped a little skip: *And then Mom will be impressed with **me.***

✳

Maryellen loved the ocean: its roar, its salty tang, and the huge blueness of it stretching all the way to the sky. "Last one in is a rotten egg!" she challenged Carolyn and Davy.

Legs pumping, arms waving, the three kids raced across the scorching sand. Maryellen plunged headfirst into an incoming wave. *Swoosh!* She had timed it just right, so that the wave lifted her up into the bright summery air. "Ya*hoo!*" Maryellen hooted exuberantly.

In a second, Carolyn popped up next to Maryellen in the water. Davy popped up next.

"What took you guys so long?" asked Maryellen, grinning.

Carolyn was grinning, too. "All right," she said. "You win, as usual."

"I guess I'm the rotten egg," said Davy. "But watch out—*someday* I'll be faster than you."

Maryellen doubted it. Davy was a pretty good runner, but Maryellen was fiercely determined when it came to running. She had had a sickness called polio when she was younger, and one leg was a little bit weaker than the other. Sometimes Maryellen worried that Mom babied her because of her leg. But Maryellen never let her leg slow her down.

It was fun to be at the beach with Davy and her brothers and sisters, but Maryellen missed Dad. He loved being at the beach, too, and always rode the waves with her. She floated in the water and looked back at the shore. Queen Beverly was building herself a sand castle under the beach umbrella. Tom and Mikey kept knocking her castle down, so after a little while, Davy got out of the water to help her by distracting them. "Hey, boys!" Davy shouted as he walked up the beach. "Let's dig a hole to China."

Joan was lying on a beach towel, reading as usual. Scooter snoozed next to her.

"Say, Joan," Carolyn called. "Come on in—the water's fine."

Joan didn't even take her eyes off her book. "No thanks," she called back.

"I bet she doesn't want to get her hair wet," Carolyn said to Maryellen. "She has a tennis date with Jerry later."

"Oooh, a date!" said Maryellen, instantly interested. Jerry was Joan's boyfriend. He went to college and had a car. Maryellen thought Jerry was a dreamboat. He reminded her of David Nelson, a college boy on *The Adventures of Ozzie and Harriet*, because he was so handsome. Even though she was still mad at Joan for the crabby, critical things she'd said that morning, Maryellen had to admit that pretty Joan and handsome Jerry were the perfect couple.

A brilliant thought came to her. If Joan married Jerry, she'd move out and go to live with him. Then she'd stop picking on Maryellen all the time—and Maryellen would have only Mom to win over about the All Girls Room.

Maryellen turned to Carolyn, who knew all about love and marriage because she was in high school, and asked, "Do you think Joan and Jerry will get married?"

"Well," said Carolyn, lighting up, "millions of girls do get married after high school. And Joan and Jerry are already going steady. The next step is for Jerry to give Joan his fraternity pin. That means they're engaged to be engaged. Then he gives her an engagement ring, and *then* comes the wedding."

"Gee," said Maryellen. "I didn't realize there were so many steps. I was sort of hoping they'd get married *soon*."

"Me too," said Carolyn. "I love weddings! I wonder if Joan would let us be bridesmaids."

"Maybe you and I could *encourage* Joan and Jerry," said Maryellen.

"How?" asked Carolyn.

"Well, first of all, we could give Jerry a little nudge,"

said Maryellen, "and tell him to hurry up and propose to Joan."

"Yikes," said Carolyn. "I'm too chicken to do *that*."

"I'm not," said Maryellen. "Jerry's not scary."

"It's not Jerry I'm scared of," said Carolyn. "It's Joan. She'd skin us alive if she found out."

"She doesn't need to know," said Maryellen. "We'll just talk to Jerry sometime when Joan's not around."

Carolyn began to say, "Joan won't—" But right then, Davy came splashing back into the water.

"Come on," he said. "Let's do backward somer-saults."

"Okay!" said Maryellen and Carolyn, putting the topic of marriage aside.

The three kids curled up with their knees under their chins and used their arms to spin themselves around backward, swirling under the water and then up into the dazzling, sunny air. One of Maryellen's favorite TV shows was a broadcast of the waterski-ing and synchronized-swimming show at Cypress Gardens, which was right in her own state of Florida. Maryellen pretended now that she was one of the Cypress Gardens mermaids, and practiced smiling for the television camera every time she came up for air after flipping and twirling underwater.

In a little while, Joan called, "Okay, kids! Time to go."

Normally, everyone would beg to stay longer. But today, Maryellen, Davy, and Carolyn ran up to the umbrella and toweled off and put their shoes on, and Beverly and the little boys picked up their sand pails and shovels and got ready to walk home without a murmur. Today Betty and Florence were coming!

Maryellen rushed to help Joan shake the sand off her beach towel and fold it neatly. Joan said nothing, but raised her eyebrows at Maryellen's unusual eagerness to be neat. Then Joan tucked her towel and book under her arm, put Mikey in his stroller, and took Tom by the hand. Carolyn, Maryellen, and Beverly hoisted the beach umbrella onto their shoulders and carried it, all in a row, with Maryellen in the middle. Davy brought up the rear, herding sluggish Scooter homeward.

The Larkins lived in a housing development in Daytona Beach called The Palms. The development had its own community pool, but the Larkin kids weren't allowed to go there for fear of catching polio. There had been a polio epidemic two years ago—that's when Maryellen had had it—and ever since then, Dad had put the kibosh on going to the community pool. It was forbidden.

Maryellen knew just about everyone who lived in the houses on her street, most of them in big families like hers. She had always liked how safe and familiar her neighborhood was, and how homey the pretty little matching houses were, all lined up in rows, facing one another cheerfully across the street. Each house had a driveway, a carport, a small lawn, and a palm tree. But suddenly, today, the sameness felt flat to Maryellen. Today, it occurred to her that The Palms might look dull to Betty and Florence. They lived in New York City, for heaven's sake! Maryellen had never been to New York, but she knew that it was an exciting, bustling big city full of action and variety. And she could tell that Mom wanted to impress Betty and Florence. How could their home be impressive if it was just like all the other houses on the street?

"You can hardly tell these houses apart," Maryellen said aloud. "About the only difference is that some houses have pink plastic flamingos on their lawns and some don't. We should do something to make *our* house stand out."

"Like what?" asked Carolyn.

"I don't know yet," said Maryellen. "But I'll think of *some*thing."

As they walked up the driveway, Maryellen thought hard about what she could do to make their house *extraordinary* instead of *extra ordinary*. Davy waved good-bye and went next door to his own house. Mom met them at the kitchen door, standing in the shade of the carport. She was wearing a dress and a hat and high-heeled sandals, and the car keys jingled in her hand. "I'm on my way to the airport to pick up Betty and Florence," Mom said.

"Wow, Mom, you look beautiful," said Maryellen. "You look just like a mother on TV." That was Maryellen's highest compliment. It worried her a little bit that most of the time, Mom distinctly did *not* look like one of the mothers on TV who vacuumed their spotless houses wearing high heels and pearls and always had a chocolate cake on hand. Instead, Mrs. Larkin usually wore sneakers, pedal pushers, and one of Dad's old shirts. But today, Maryellen saw that Mom's fingernails and toenails had fire-engine-red polish on them. They were as red and shiny and eye-popping as Mom's red lipstick. Now Maryellen was absolutely positive: Mom *really* wanted to impress Betty and Florence. Oh, she ached to help Mom do just that!

That's when Maryellen had a great idea about how to snazz up their house. She thought of a surefire way that she, all by herself, could make their house stand out from every other house on the street. She couldn't *wait* to make it happen.

Meanwhile, Mrs. Larkin was saying, "Thank you, darlings. Everything is spick-and-span and perfect for Betty and Florence, and I want it to stay that way. So everyone, please hose off your feet before you go inside. I don't want you tracking sand all over my clean kitchen floor."

"Okay, Mom," said everybody automatically.

"What smells so good?" asked Carolyn.

"Oh, I'm glad you reminded me," said Mom, a little bit flustered. "There are brownies in the oven. Take them out when the timer dings, okay? But don't eat any."

"Okay, Mom," said everybody automatically again. Maryellen was so excited about her idea that she wasn't really paying much attention.

"Well, all right. I'd better go," said Mrs. Larkin. She got in the car. As she drove off, she waved and called out the window, "Be good."

"Okay, Mom," said everybody one more time.

Hurray, thought Maryellen, happy and excited. *Mom's finally gone. Now I can work on my surprise.*

Extraordinary, Not Extra Ordinary

✶ CHAPTER THREE ✶

he hose was right next to the kitchen door. Tom, who always liked to pretend that he was a fireman, held the hose while Joan washed the sand off Mikey's feet, which made Mikey giggle and dance. Then Tom squirted Scooter, who sat agreeably and let him do it.

Maryellen didn't even change out of her bathing suit, but went straight to the carport and began rummaging around on Dad's workbench for red paint and a paintbrush. She was going to paint the front door of their house red, *really* red: bright, shiny, eye-catching, fingernail-polish-ish, lipstick-y red. No one else in The Palms had a red front door! Betty and Florence would be so impressed. They'd say to Mom, "My goodness, Kay! Your house really stands out from the rest. It's extraordinary! It's the only one with a bright red door!"

And Mom would smile proudly and say, "Maryellen painted our door red. It was her idea. She always has great ideas!" And *then*, when Betty and Florence talked to Maryellen for the first time, they wouldn't say what people *usually* said, which was, "You're Maryellen? Which one are you, the second, third, or fourth sister?" Instead, they would say, "You're *Maryellen*? Oh! You're the one with all the great ideas!"

Maryellen was so intent on imagining Mom's pride and Betty's and Florence's admiration, and so focused on her search for paint, that she practically jumped a foot when Beverly's squeaky voice behind her asked, "What are you doing?"

Maryellen turned to see Beverly, Tom, Mikey, and Scooter standing in a row behind her, watching her. Beverly was wearing her baseball-cap crown. Except for Scooter, they were all eating orange Popsicles, so their mouths were wreathed in orange stickiness.

"What are you doing?" asked Beverly again.

"Nothing," Maryellen answered. "Go find Carolyn."

"She left for her piano lesson," said Beverly. "She said to tell you to take the brownies out."

"What about Joan?" said Maryellen.

"She's getting ready for Jerry," said Beverly. "She gave us Popsicles and told us to come find you."

Maryellen sighed. She could see that she was stuck with Beverly, Tom, Mikey, and Scooter as an audience for her project whether she liked it or not. "All right," she said briskly. "I'm going to paint the front door red, like Mom's fingernail polish. You can watch. But don't get in the way."

Maryellen found a can of red paint and a paintbrush left over from when Dad had touched up Tom's fire truck. The paint was sort of lumpy and smelly, and the brush had dried so that it was stiffened into a hard curve. Maryellen knew that Dad would say that she should clean the brush with turpentine, but she didn't have time to fuss. She had to finish her surprise before Mom and Betty and Florence came home. To make herself faster and taller, Maryellen put on her roller skates. She pictured herself gliding smoothly as she painted, like the waitresses on roller skates at drive-up restaurants she had seen on TV.

"I want to paint, too," said Beverly. She and Mikey trailed along behind Maryellen as she roller-skated to the front door. Scooter, who had an unerring instinct about where he'd be most in the way, plunked himself down right behind Maryellen.

"I want to paint, too," echoed Tom, pedaling his fire engine along behind them.

"Paint!" said Mikey.

"No," said Maryellen.

"Why?" asked Beverly.

"Because there's only one brush."

"Can I have a turn with it?" asked Beverly.

"Me, too?" asked Tom.

"Paint!" said Mikey.

"No," said Maryellen shortly.

"Why not?" asked Beverly.

"Because it was my idea and I'm doing it," said Maryellen. She sounded crosser than she meant to. The truth was that she was cross at *herself*, because only now that she looked at the front door did she realize that she had forgotten about the screen door, which was outside the front door, so she'd have to paint that first.

Oh, well. There's not much to paint. How hard could it be? Maryellen thought. She remembered seeing a commercial on television in which a lady painted her whole living room all by herself, and there was nothing to it! She pretended to be in that TV commercial. She held the can of paint in one hand, dipped the brush into it, and boldly swiped a stroke of red on the middle slat of the screen door.

"Uh-oh," said Beverly.

"Uh-oh what?" asked Maryellen, even though she had spotted a problem, too.

"It's all bumpy," said Beverly.

"Oh, no one will see," said Maryellen airily, even though it was easy to see that she'd painted over dead bugs, and their bodies were now permanently attached to the screen door, like raised polka dots. She was glad when Joan's boyfriend, Jerry, drove up in his convertible hot rod. He would be a great distraction for her critical audience.

"Hi, Jerry!" Maryellen, Beverly, and Tom called. Maryellen turned and waved her paintbrush.

"Hi, kids," said Jerry as he got out of his car and came up the front walk. Maryellen thought he looked very handsome in his white tennis outfit. "What's with the paint, Ellie?"

"Paint!" said Mikey.

"I'm painting our door red," Maryellen explained. "It's a surprise for Mom."

"She'll be surprised, all right," said Jerry. "I guess I'd better knock on the kitchen door, to let Joan know I'm here for our date."

Maryellen seized the opportunity, even though she knew she was risking Joan's wrath. "Speaking of dates," she said to Jerry, "have you ever thought about *setting* a date? To marry Joan, I mean."

"To—to what?" Jerry sputtered. He looked surprised.

"Marry Joan," Maryellen plowed on doggedly. "She's almost eighteen, you know. She'll graduate from high school next June. And millions of girls get married right after they graduate."

Jerry looked stunned, as if someone had bonked him on the noggin. He was speechless.

Maryellen pressed on. "You had better ask her soon," she advised Jerry. "She's awfully pretty, and very popular, and—" But Maryellen didn't have a chance to finish her sentence, because just then, everything happened at once.

Beverly, who had been dipping her empty Popsicle stick into the paint can and painting her fingernails red, stopped and looked up. "Ellie," she asked, "what's that smell?"

Maryellen turned and saw smoke billowing out of the kitchen door just as Carolyn came running up the driveway waving her piano music and shouting, "Ellie! The brownies—they're burning!"

Joan, rushing out to see what the fuss was, flung open the front screen door and knocked Maryellen backward on her roller skates. As Maryellen fell over Scooter and landed bottom-first in a bush, red paint went flying—all over her, all over the front step, and all over Jerry's white tennis shorts and shirt.

"Hey!" exclaimed Jerry.

"Oh *no!*" shrieked Joan.

Tom, making siren noises and clanging the bell on his fire truck, pedaled to the kitchen door and turned on the hose. He squirted water through the kitchen screen door, trying to put out the fire in the oven like a fireman. Beverly held up her hands, which were covered in red paint, and wailed. Mikey, unperturbed, picked up the paintbrush and began painting red stripes on Scooter, who didn't seem to mind.

And it was at that exact moment that Mrs. Larkin's

car pulled into the driveway, horn honking *"Honk, honk!"* to announce its happy arrival.

"MOM!" Joan, Carolyn, Maryellen, Beverly, and Tom yelled at the top of their lungs.

"Fire!" yelled Jerry.

"Paint!" yelled Mikey.

"Ar-oooo!" howled Scooter, not to be left out of the ruckus. *"Ar-ooo! Ar-ooo! Ar-ooo!"*

The car screeched to a stop, and Mrs. Larkin, Betty, and Florence jumped out.

"What's going on?" Mrs. Larkin shouted, over and above all the noise. "Oh, my stars—look at this mess! How on earth did this happen?"

Suddenly, everyone was quiet. None of them had ever seen Mom this mad before. Even Scooter was cowed, and maintained a dignified silence.

Maryellen stepped forward. At this moment, she certainly had her mother's undivided attention, and oh boy, did she ever wish she *didn't.* "Mom," she began. Her voice sounded as wobbly as her knees felt. "I was only trying to paint the door. I didn't mean to make a mess. I'm sorry."

"Sorry?" Joan repeated. "You've ruined Jerry's

tennis clothes. You've ruined our date. You've ruined the front of our house. And all you can say is you're *sorry*?" Joan put her hands on her hips and leaned toward Maryellen. "This is just the kind of disaster I was talking about earlier. Mom lets you get away with murder, but you're not a baby anymore! When are you going to grow up?" She stormed off with Jerry, holding him by the arm, but gingerly, so that she wouldn't get red paint on her tennis dress.

"Oh, Ellie," moaned Mom. She closed her eyes and pressed her red fingertips to her forehead. Then she opened her eyes and said, "Ellie, I will speak to you about this privately. Carolyn, please help Betty and Florence get settled, and then give them a glass of iced tea on the back patio."

"Sure, Mom," said Carolyn. Everyone skedaddled, and Jerry and Joan drove away. Mom and Maryellen were alone.

Maryellen picked up the paintbrush and the paint can and tried to explain. "I only wanted to—"

But Mom interrupted. "No explanations right now, please. And just leave the mess," she said flatly. "We'll deal with it later, after Betty and Florence have left.

Right this very minute, I've got to tell you that I am disappointed in you. Dad would be, too. It is childish to get so carried away that you don't stop to think. I understand that in a big family like ours, it's hard to get your fair share of attention. But Ellie, honey, like it or not, you are just one of six children. You cannot be the center of attention all the time. And in any case, there are better ways of getting attention than showing off and slathering red paint all over. Didn't you promise me just this morning that you'd act more responsibly?"

Maryellen nodded. She was too close to tears to speak. She was sorry to have upset Mom, and she was even sorrier that her surefire way of pleasing Mom had completely backfired. What a flop! What a failure! What a *disaster*.

She sure had failed Mom's test. Now Joan and Mom would *never* agree to the All Girls Room. Worse than that, instead of thinking that she was more grown-up, Mom and Joan now thought of her as even more messy and irresponsible than before.

✳

The full moon was so bright and shone such a strong silver light into the bedroom that Maryellen could not sleep. Lying on her upper bunk, she tossed and turned and flushed hot and cold just *thinking* of the red paint disaster. No one had said anything about it at dinner or later while everyone was watching TV. Even Joan didn't mention it, and her silence was strange considering how mad she'd been earlier. But Maryellen knew it was on everyone's mind. Especially *hers*.

"Jeez Louise, Ellie," Joan said sleepily. "Stop spinning around. What are you doing—practicing your underwater somersaults? Go to sleep, why don't you?"

"Sorry," said Maryellen. She flinched, expecting Joan to jump all over her again the way she had earlier when Maryellen had used the inadequate word *sorry*.

But Joan didn't. In fact, her voice was kind when she said, "Listen, Ellie-jelly, don't be so hard on yourself. You're upset because your red paint idea didn't work out. But everybody makes a mistake once in a while. Your mistake today just happened to be a lulu."

"*All* my ideas seem to be mistakes," said Maryellen. "They're *all* lulus."

"Oh, I don't know about that," said Joan. "You had

one good idea today."

"I did?" asked Maryellen. She could hardly believe her ears. "What was it?"

Joan giggled a little. "You told Jerry to, uh, get on the ball," she said.

Maryellen gulped. "You're not mad about that?" she asked.

"Well, no," said Joan. "In fact, I'm glad you said something."

Maryellen was flabbergasted. "Glad?" she repeated.

"Mm-hmm," said Joan. "Thanks to you, Jerry finally gave me his fraternity pin."

"He did?" squeaked Maryellen.

"Yep," said Joan. "I was hoping that he would pin me before he went back to college in the fall, but of course I couldn't ask him. *Girls* don't propose to *boys*."

"So that means you're engaged to be engaged, right?" Maryellen asked. "And does *that* mean you'll be getting married soon?" Now that Joan was being so nice, Maryellen wasn't sure she wanted her to leave—not right away, at least.

"No, we won't be getting married for a while yet," said Joan. "So don't say anything to Mom and Dad.

Jerry and I want to talk to them together, because it's a pretty big deal. Getting pinned *does* mean there's a wedding in our future."

"Oh boy!" said Maryellen. "A wedding! Can I help you plan it?"

"You bet," said Joan. "So, see? Not all of your ideas are bombs. Even this All Girls Room isn't as bad as I thought it would be. I have more space in here, and you organized your stuff pretty well. After Betty and Florence leave, I think I'll tell Mom it's okay with me to make the move permanent."

"Really?" asked Maryellen, her heart lifting.

"Really," said Joan. She yawned, and then she said, "You still have to get Mom to agree, though. Now if you could just come up with another one of your Great Ideas for undoing the mess you made with the red paint out front, you'd be all set. Meanwhile, go to sleep, okay?"

"Okay, I'll try," said Maryellen. Full of gratitude for Joan's forgiveness, she closed her eyes and tried to go to sleep. But her brain kept going over and over what Joan had said. *Undo the mess, undo the mess . . . How,* Maryellen thought, *can I undo the mess?*

In the Pink

✻ CHAPTER FOUR ✻

aryellen's eyes popped open. She slid out of bed and quietly, quietly, ever so quietly, she tiptoed outside into the balmy Florida night. She skittered over the grass in her bare feet and slid through the hedge that divided her yard from Davy's.

*Tap, tappety, tap, tap. Tap, **tap***. Maryellen used her fingernail to beat their secret signal on Davy's bedroom window.

After a moment, Davy appeared. He took one look at Maryellen and climbed out his window. "What's up, Doc?" he whispered.

Maryellen held one finger to her lips to signal *quiet*. With the other hand, she gestured to Davy to follow her.

The moon cast Davy's and Maryellen's shadows ahead of them as she led the way to the garage and to Dad's workbench. She handed Davy the can of red paint and the paintbrush, and then gathered rags, a scrub brush, and the tin of turpentine in her own arms. She led Davy to the front of the house.

"Holy cow," breathed Davy when he saw the mess. "What happened here?"

"It's a long story," Maryellen sighed sadly. "Anyway, would you mind painting the doors while I scrub the step?"

"Sure," said Davy without hesitation. He began to say, "Let's—" But just then Scooter, who had been banished from the house because his stripes of red paint were still wet, ambled into view. "Holy *cow*!" Davy exclaimed softly. "Get a load of Scooter! Stripes, for Pete's sake!"

"Hi, old boy," Maryellen said to Scooter. "I'm afraid your shampoo will have to wait. You'll have those red stripes until tomorrow." Scooter didn't seem to mind. In fact, Maryellen thought he seemed rather pleased to have red stripes, as if he were a sporty, portly tiger.

The front of the house was bathed in moonlight. As Davy finished painting the screen door and started on the front door, Maryellen soaked her rags in turpentine and scrubbed and scrubbed. It was hard work to remove the red paint from the front step. How had it splattered so far and wide? She wouldn't have thought there was quite so much red paint in the world, much less in that one can. The turpentine had a sharp smell that made her eyes and nose run. But Maryellen did not give up.

Davy, on the other hand, seemed to enjoy painting. "Hey, let's pretend we're in an episode of a TV show about pirates," he suggested.

"Or how about if we're explorers," said Maryellen, perking up, "and we were sailing the seven seas when we were *captured* by the pirates? They make us work day and night! You're painting the mast, and I'm swabbing the decks of the pirate ship. But pretty soon, with our brave companion, Sea Wolf—that's Scooter—we'll jump overboard and swim away."

"Good idea," said Davy. "Ahoy there, Sea Wolf!"

Scooter thumped his tail, to show that he was in on the game.

Pretending helped the time go faster, but it still felt to Maryellen as though she was scrubbing for hours. Scrubbing was very humbling work. Her knees hurt, her arm was sore, and her hands felt rubbed raw.

At last, most of the splattered red paint was gone. Maryellen thought the step looked a bit pinkish, but perhaps it was just a trick of the moonlight. Davy finished painting the doors, and then he and Maryellen wiped their hands on the turpentine rags and washed them with the hose. Maryellen dried her hands on her pajama bottoms, and Davy used his T-shirt.

When his hands were dry, Davy saluted and said quietly, "Anchors aweigh, matey."

Maryellen saluted back. She sure hoped Joan was wrong about not being friends with a boy in fourth grade. Davy was such a good pal. "Anchors aweigh," she said. "And Davy, thank you."

Davy grinned. "Any time," he said. He stooped over to give Scooter a quick pat—Scooter opened one eye, briefly—and then Davy zipped home.

Maryellen sneaked back to bed, tired and smelling of turpentine.

✳

The next morning, Mom woke Maryellen with a kiss. She opened her eyes to see Mom smiling at her. "Hey, Ellie," Mom said softly. "Are you the magic fairy who scrubbed away the red paint?"

Maryellen nodded. "And Davy painted the doors," she said.

"Well, thanks," said Mom. "That was a big job. And that's what I call taking responsibility. You're forgiven for yesterday. I rather like having a red door and a pink step out front. I bet Dad will like them, too! Come on, let's have breakfast. Betty is making pancakes. Want some?"

"Yes, *ma'am*," said Maryellen. She hugged Mom hard for a moment and then bounced out of bed. She was so happy and relieved that she practically flew into the kitchen.

When Maryellen watched Mom, Betty, and Florence together, they reminded *her* of magic fairies. They finished one another's sentences and all talked at the same time and laughed and laughed and laughed. They sang while they washed the breakfast dishes. They cooked up delicious fudgy brownies that were *not* burnt, and filled the house with enchanting, warm, chocolatey smells, using spoons instead of magic wands to cast a spell of happiness.

After breakfast, Mom and Betty and Florence got

all dolled up. Mom was wearing a hat and gloves, and Maryellen noticed with admiration that her purse matched her high heels. Betty and Florence put their suitcases in the car because they were taking the train to visit friends in Miami after the reunion. As Mom and her friends drove off, Mom waved out the car window and called, "Bye, kids! Ellie, please, no surprises when I get back. Promise?"

"I promise," said Maryellen.

With Mom, Betty, and Florence gone, the house felt dull. Everybody cheered up a bit when Joan said that they could have brownies for dessert for lunch, as long as they saved one for Dad, who loved brownies. Still, they were all glad to see Mom when she got home at about three o'clock.

"Was the reunion luncheon fun?" Maryellen asked Mom. She wondered if seeing her old coworkers made Mom wish she were still the star of the factory.

"Yes, it was," said Mom as she kicked off her high heels and took off her hat. "It was lovely to see everyone again. But do you know, Betty and Florence said that they had more fun here at our house. They said it was far more entertaining than the reunion."

Mom winked at Maryellen, who blushed. "Betty and Florence got a big kick out of you kids. They told me that Dad and I are lucky to have such a lively, rowdy family." Mom hugged Mikey and tousled Tom's hair. "And I think they're exactly right."

"Well," said Joan. "*Most* of the time."

And everyone—even Maryellen—laughed.

✳

The next day, Maryellen was in her bedroom sketching bride dresses and hairdos when Mom popped her head in and said, "I checked, and just as I suspected, you *do* need new socks and underwear. How would you like to go shopping today?"

"Sure," said Maryellen.

"All right then," said Mom. "There's no time like the present. Let's go!"

So, just like *that*, Maryellen found herself skipping happily through the shopping center parking lot next to Mom, trying to keep up with her mother's long strides. She was excited and delighted to be on a shopping trip, even if it *was* only for underwear and *not* for a new dress to wear on the first day of school instead of

Carolyn's plaid hand-me-down. That didn't matter. The important thing was that today, for a few hours at least, Maryellen had Mom *all to herself.*

Maryellen and Mom walked into the cool of O'Neal's, the nicest department store at the shopping center, and rode the stately silver escalator up to the Girls' Department on the second floor. As Maryellen stepped off the escalator, she came to a sudden stop. There on a mannequin, right before her very eyes, was the most wonderful outfit she had ever seen. It was a white blouse, a black patent leather belt, and a very, very full black felt skirt with a pink poodle appliqué on it.

"Oh, Mom, *look*," said Maryellen exuberantly. "A poodle skirt!" She touched the poodle's shiny black button eyes and traced the loops of its leash. "Isn't this the cutest outfit in the world?"

"It's cute," said Mom briskly. "But we're here for underwear."

"Yes, of course," said Maryellen. Dutifully, she followed Mom to the underwear section and tried to be enthusiastic about white cotton undershirts and bobby socks. Talk about dull! Socks were socks and all the same!

"While we're here, let's get underwear for Tom and Dad, too," said Mom.

Maryellen swallowed a groan. Underwear for boys and men was even more boring than underwear for girls. But she was patient as Mom chose underpants for Tom and boxer shorts for Dad. And she was patient while she and Mom waited in line to pay for their purchases at the checkout counter, though she couldn't help looking longingly over her shoulder at the poodle skirt in the Girls' Department. A small, sad sigh escaped her.

Mom heard the sigh, and saw what Maryellen was gazing at. "Ellie, sweetie," Mom said, with a note of warning in her voice, "we're not shopping for skirts today, remember? You already have a perfectly fine back-to-school dress—the plaid one from Carolyn. Didn't we agree on that?"

"Yes," said Maryellen. Mom was right: The plaid dress was perfectly fine. It was just so very *ordinary*. She knew that she should not bug Mom about the fabulous poodle skirt, but . . . She gathered her courage, and asked, "Mom, what if I just zipped over to the Girls' Department and tried on the skirt while you're waiting here in line?"

"Well, all right," said Mrs. Larkin. "But I won't be long, so don't dillydally."

"I won't," Maryellen promised. She grabbed a skirt in her size off the rack, rushed to a dressing room, and tried the skirt on over her sundress. If anything, she thought the poodle skirt looked even *more* wonderful than she'd expected. She twirled around in front of the three dressing-room mirrors to make the skirt swing out in a perfect circle, and she was delighted to see hundreds of twirling Maryellens reflected around her in a swirling *swoosh*.

Mom poked her head in around the dressing-room curtain. "Ready to go?" she asked.

Maryellen nodded.

Mom looked at Maryellen and raised an eyebrow. "My, but the poodle on that skirt is *pink*," she said dryly. "And pink is a color that I should think you'd like to avoid today—even to try on. Your hands are still a bit pink from scrubbing away all that red paint."

"Oh, Mom," Maryellen burst out. "You were right— I *did* paint the front door red to show off and get attention for myself. But I also painted it for you. I thought that if our house looked special, your friends would be impressed. They'd see how special *you* are."

"Oh," said Mom. She stepped into the dressing room and sat down hard on the little stool next to the mirror. "Really?" she asked.

Maryellen nodded. "Yes!" she said fervently. "I didn't want our house to look boring and ordinary, because I didn't want Betty and Florence to think that we were boring and ordinary—especially not *you*."

"I see," said Mom. "You were feeling overlooked and underappreciated, and you thought I was, too. So you wanted to make a big splash for both of us."

Maryellen winced at the word *splash*, but said, "Yes."

"I see," said Mom again. "I'm glad I understand better now. It was sweet of you to think of me and how I might be feeling. And it was good of you to scrub off the red paint, too. I know that was hard work. You made a mess, but you took responsibility for cleaning it up."

"And it was actually Joan who sort of gave me the idea," said Maryellen.

"Did she?" said Mom. "It sounds like she's forgiven you for splattering red paint on Jerry."

Maryellen smiled and shrugged. She knew the reason why Joan had forgiven her, but Joan had asked her not to tell Mom about being pinned, so she kept quiet.

"Anyway, you seem to be back in Joan's good graces," Mom went on. "If she gives her approval to the All Girls Room, then as far as I'm concerned, it's a done deal. You can help Joan and Carolyn move in permanently when we get home."

"Really, Mom?" Maryellen asked. "I'm pretty sure Joan likes it. At least, she told me she did."

Mom stood up, crossed her arms, tilted her head, and observed Maryellen from head to toe. "All of a sudden, you're looking more mature to me, Miss Maryellen Larkin," she said. "And I don't think it's just because of that very chic poodle skirt you're wearing, either."

Maryellen beamed.

"In fact, the more I look at it, the more I think that skirt suits you," said Mom. "It's quite grown-up, and you are, too. Dad would say that you look like a million bucks in it! Ellie-girl, I think you've found yourself a very glamorous back-to-school skirt, don't you? Let's buy it."

✳ In the Pink ✳

Maryellen gasped. She threw herself at Mom and said, "Oh, thank you, Mom! Thank you, thank you, *thank* you. I love it!"

Maryellen was thrilled. The poodle skirt would be one of the first *new* things, and certainly one of the most *beautiful* things, she'd ever owned in her life! It was fun and fancy and fashionable. She was absolutely sure that the poodle skirt guaranteed she'd have not only a great first day of school, but also a great *year* in fourth grade.

Even better, the poodle skirt was a perfect reminder that Mom didn't think of her as a little kid anymore, but as someone more grown-up, whose ideas should be taken seriously. After all, even if *some* of her great ideas did not work out as perfectly as they did in her imaginary TV shows, *some*how *some*times *some* things still ended happily, just as they had today.

The thought of happy endings reminded Maryellen of her Jerry-and-Joan Wedding Project. "Say, Mom," she asked casually, "on our way out of the store, may we swing though the Bridal Shop?"

"Sure!" said Mom. "That's a great idea. It'll be fun."

Oh boy! thought Maryellen. *A poodle skirt, the All*

Girls Room, fourth grade . . . and a wedding to look forward to! The months to come were sure to be **extra** extraordinary!

Being Noticed

ap, tappety, tap, tap. Tap, **tap**.

Maryellen knocked on Davy's front door the next morning, using their secret signal.

Davy opened the door right away. "What's up, Doc?" he said, pretending to be Bugs Bunny as usual.

"Want to ride bikes?" Maryellen asked.

"Sure," said Davy.

Maryellen and Davy both leaped from the front step to the grass, and then Davy headed to the carport to get his bike. Maryellen's bike was parked on the Fenstermachers' driveway, guarded by roly-poly Scooter, who liked any job that did not require moving. Maryellen hopped on her bike and practiced popping wheelies on Davy's driveway, raising the front tire of her bike off the pavement as if her bike were a horse rearing up on its hind legs and she was the solo star of a rodeo with a spotlight shining on her.

"Hi-yo, Silver! Awaa-a-ay!" shouted Davy as he careened toward Maryellen on his bike. Then he popped a wheelie, too.

Maryellen laughed. She knew that Davy was pretending to be the Lone Ranger, because Silver was the name of the Lone Ranger's horse.

"Let's ride, pardner," she said.

But Maryellen and Davy had ridden no farther than the end of the driveway before a boy named Wayne rode up on his bike, so they reined to a halt.

"Hey, Fenstermacher," said Wayne to Davy, ignoring Maryellen. "My dad just put up a basketball hoop. Want to go shoot baskets?"

"Sure," said Davy. "Want to come, Ellie?"

"Okay," she said, even though she didn't especially like Wayne, who treated her as if she were invisible. She didn't especially like basketball, either, but she knew that Davy was crazy about it.

Wayne looked sideways at Maryellen, as if he had just noticed that she was there. "Think you'll be able to keep up with us with your gimpy leg, and on that baby bike?"

Maryellen flushed as she always did when anyone

mentioned her polio. She *never* let her weaker leg slow
her down. As for her bike, well, it *was* an old clunker
with fat tires like a little kid's bike. Davy and Wayne
had sleek black bikes with thin tires, three gears, and
brakes on the handlebars. Her bike had rusty handlebars, a broken bell, a battered basket, and no front
fender. Joan had handed it down to Carolyn, who had
handed it down to Maryellen, who had almost outgrown it herself by now.

"Don't worry," said Davy. "Ellie's bike only looks
slow until she starts to pedal it."

Maryellen gave him a grateful grin. Good old Davy!
He always stood up for her.

Wayne shrugged. He began to say, "Well—"

But then Beverly pedaled up on her tricycle, calling, "Wait!" As usual, Beverly was an eyeful. It was
impossible to ignore *her.* She was wearing a glittery
belt wrapped around her waist twice, a necklace made
of shells, rhinestone-studded sunglasses, and her
inside-out baseball-cap crown. A box of animal crackers dangled from her wrist as a pretend purse. When
Scooter got a whiff of the animal crackers, he rose to
his feet slowly and waddled over to investigate.

"Ellie, wait," Beverly said. "I'm coming too."

"No, I don't think so, shrimp," said Wayne.

Maryellen and Davy rolled their eyes at each other. Wayne didn't know Beverly very well, so he didn't know that saying no to Beverly was usually useless. Mr. Larkin didn't call her "Queen Beverly" only because she dressed up as a queen; she *acted* majestic, too, and insisted on being included in whatever fun Maryellen was having.

Maryellen saw Beverly preparing to explode, so she said quickly, "Davy and Wayne, you guys go."

"Bye!" said Wayne, making a hasty getaway.

"Thanks, Ellie," said Davy, shooting her an apologetic look for leaving her behind as he followed Wayne.

"Come on, Beverly," said Maryellen. "I'll race you and Scooter home."

Scooter, who had gone to sleep, yawned and got to his feet in slow motion.

"Uh-oh, looks like speedy Scooter plans to leave us in the dust," Maryellen joked. "Ready, Beverly? On your mark, get set, *go*."

✳

✳ Being Noticed ✳

Maryellen often thought she was the luckiest girl in the world, because she had *three* best friends. There was Davy right next door, of course, and then she also had two best girlfriends. If that wasn't fun enough, both girls were named Karen! One was Karen Stohlman and one was Karen King. Maryellen mostly saw the Karens at school, because they lived in a different neighborhood. When summer vacation ended and school started again, she and her three best friends were going to be in fourth grade together.

One afternoon shortly before the first day of school, Karen Stohlman's mother drove the two Karens over to Maryellen's house to play. Mr. Larkin had painted permanent hopscotch squares on the driveway, so the girls were having a hopscotch marathon.

Maryellen tossed her marker, which was an old Popsicle stick, and hopped to the square it landed on, talking at the same time. "I hope Mrs. (hop) Humphrey (hop) is nice (hop, hop, hop)," she said. "Joan and Carolyn had her as their teacher when they were in fourth grade, and they liked her a lot."

Karen Stohlman, who took ballet, rose up on tiptoe and twirled so fast that her long brown ponytail stuck straight out from her head. "I'm so glad the three of us are all in the same class," she said.

"And Davy's in our class, too," Maryellen reminded her, "so this is going to be our best school year ever. I just know it."

"Yes!" said Karen King. Her round, freckly face looked cheerful. "Plus this year we finally get to be Girl Scouts."

"Hurray!" cheered Maryellen, and Karen Stohlman twirled again. Maryellen, Karen, and Karen had liked being Brownies well enough, but they'd been looking forward to being Girl Scouts for years.

"We'll be the *most outstanding* Girl Scouts ever," said Maryellen. "We'll earn *more* merit badges than anyone else, and sell the *most* Girl Scout cookies, and have the *most* fun on the hikes."

"We can sleep in the same tent on the overnight camping trips," said Karen Stohlman.

"And," Maryellen added joyfully, "instead of boring Brownie brown, our uniforms will be gen-u-ine Girl Scout green."

"Do you two have your uniforms yet?" asked Karen Stohlman.

"Yes," said Maryellen and Karen King.

"Me too," said Karen Stohlman. "Mine was a little too long, so my mom's hemming it." She didn't say so, but Maryellen knew that Karen Stohlman's Girl Scout uniform was brand-new. She had only an older brother, so all her clothes were new. "You know what's going to be great?" Karen continued. "When we all wear our uniforms, we'll look exactly alike. We'll be triplets!"

"Uh, not exactly," said Maryellen. "My uniform is a hand-me-down. First Joan wore it, then Carolyn. It's so old that it's different from the new ones. It has long sleeves."

"Oh," said Karen Stohlman, sounding disappointed. She always liked the girls to be the *same.*

"My uniform is a hand-me-down, too," sighed Karen King, "from my sister Kathy. She's really hard on her clothes. They look like they've been through a hurricane by the time I get them."

"I know what you mean," said Maryellen. "My clothes go through both Joan and Carolyn before they come to me. And I'm supposed to be careful, because after me, my clothes go to Beverly."

"I wish I had only an older brother, like you," Karen

King said to Karen Stohlman. "You have all the luck."

"All the *worst* luck," Karen Stohlman protested. "My brother is a pain."

"My brothers are sort of cute," said Maryellen.

"That's because they're little," said Karen Stohlman.

"Davy's our age and *he's* not a pain," said Maryellen.

"Well, he's the only boy in the world who's *not*," said Karen Stohlman. "I wish I could swap my brother for a sister."

Karen King and Maryellen smiled sympathetically, and Maryellen thought that even with handed-down bikes and Girl Scout uniforms, it wasn't so bad to be part of her big family.

Furthermore, Maryellen thought with a *zing* of excitement, not *all* of her clothes were previously worn. The Karens did not know that just a few days ago, she and her mother had gone on their shopping trip and bought the wonderful, new, full-circle felt skirt with a pink French poodle on it for her to wear on the first day of fourth grade. Maryellen was privately convinced that her poodle skirt was the most gorgeous skirt in the world. *Everyone* would notice her when she wore it. She had been planning to keep her skirt a secret and to surprise Karen and Karen with it on the first day of school, but she was so excited about it that she thought she might pop.

"Guess what?" Maryellen said to the Karens. "Mom and I went shopping together, just the two of us, at O'Neal's, and now I have something brand-new, *really* new, to wear on the first day of school!"

"You went to O'Neal's?" gasped Karen King. "You lucky duck!"

"What did you get?" asked Karen Stohlman.

"Well, it's a . . ." Maryellen stopped. The poodle skirt was simply too wonderful to describe in mere words. To be fully appreciated, it had to be seen in all its pink-poodle glory. "Come on inside," she said impulsively, "so you can see it."

The three girls dropped their markers like hot potatoes and stampeded inside. Scooter followed at a more dignified pace. Maryellen led her friends to her room. There, carefully displayed on a chair, was her poodle skirt.

Both Karens gasped in appreciation.

"Isn't it the cutest skirt you've ever seen?" asked Maryellen.

"Yes!" said Karen Stohlman. "I wish I had one, too!"

"On the first day of school, I'm going to wear a pink blouse that Carolyn gave me," said Maryellen, "and I'm going to borrow Carolyn's crinoline, to make the skirt stick out."

"Goll-lee," sighed Karen King. "Ellie Larkin, you'll be the most fashionable girl in the fourth grade. Everybody will be impressed. You'll be the one-and-only girl who looks like a movie star." Karen pointed to the photos of Maryellen's favorite movie star, Debbie Reynolds, which Maryellen had taped to her mirror next to sketches of hairdos that she had drawn. "Except for your hair, you'll look exactly like Debbie Reynolds."

Maryellen beamed. She held the poodle skirt to her waist and twirled around, saying, "I can't wait to wear it on the first day of school."

"If I had one, I'd wear it *every* day of school," said Karen Stohlman. "And Saturdays and Sundays, too! It's so grown-up."

"Put it on so we can see how it fits," said Karen King.

"Okay!" said Maryellen.

But just then Tom stuck his head in the door. "Mrs. Stohlman's here," he said.

"Oh, no, we've got to go," said Karen King, turning to leave. "Well, see you on the first day of school."

"Yes!" said Maryellen. "Davy and I will ride our bikes like always, and I'll meet you on the playground. See you later, alligator!"

"See you soon, raccoon," said the Karens. "Bye!"

After the girls left, Maryellen practically danced in to dinner, filled with happy anticipation. This was going to be the best school year ever.

Unique

O n the first day of school, Maryellen woke up very early. *This is it!* she thought with a shiver of nervousness.

She tried to lie still in her top bunk. Maryellen, Carolyn, and even Queen Beverly had learned the hard way that Joan was very cross and snappish if she was awakened one minute too early. Maryellen knew that her parents were already up, because she could smell coffee, bacon, and toast and hear the soft, low murmur of Dad's voice and Mom's answering muffled laughter.

Silently, Maryellen sat up in bed. She could see her gorgeous poodle skirt waiting for her, draped neatly on the chair next to the mirror that was surrounded by photos of movie stars and sketches of hairdos. Yesterday, the last day of summer vacation, Carolyn had very nicely ironed her hand-me-down pink blouse, so it was crisp and fresh-looking on its hanger. While Carolyn ironed, Maryellen had polished a pair of oxfords she had inherited from Carolyn, so they looked brown and shiny and ready to go.

Finally, Maryellen couldn't wait a moment longer. She anchored her feet between the mattress and the wall and dangled her head and arms off the top bunk so that she could tug on Carolyn's pillow.

"Carolyn!" she whispered. "Are you awake?"

"Yes," said Carolyn right away.

"Let's get up and get dressed," said Maryellen. "First dibs on the bathroom."

"Okay," said Carolyn. "But be quiet. Don't wake up Joan."

Maryellen hopped down to the floor and pulled up her sheets and blankets in a slapdash effort to make her bed. She tiptoed to the bathroom and splashed water on her face so hurriedly that a lot of her hair got wet. Then she rushed back to the bedroom.

"Thanks for letting me borrow your crinoline," Maryellen said softly as Carolyn helped her slip it on over her head. The crinoline would go under the skirt to make it puff out a bit more.

"You're welcome," said Carolyn, who seemed almost as excited about the poodle skirt as Maryellen was. At fourteen, Carolyn was quite a bit taller than Maryellen, so they had to pull the crinoline up to Maryellen's armpits to keep it from hanging below the hem of the poodle skirt.

"I'm like a bride," joked Maryellen. "I've got something old—my shoes—and something new—my skirt—and something borrowed—your crinoline. All I need is something blue."

"Well, what color's your underwear?" asked Carolyn.

For some reason, this made both Maryellen and Carolyn dissolve into giggles. They clamped their hands over their mouths to stifle their laughter, which of course only made them giggle harder.

"Ohh, honestly!" moaned Joan, rising up from her pillow, looking cranky. "You two are about as quiet as cackling hens. I can hear you, snorting like Scooter." She propped herself up on her elbow and scrutinized Maryellen. "Pretty good, Ellie-deli," she said. "But your hair should be in a ponytail. And the shoes are all wrong. Poodle skirts go with sneakers or saddle shoes, not oxfords." Then she yawned, sank back into her pillow, and seemed to go back to sleep.

Maryellen and Carolyn stared down at the clunky brown oxfords on Maryellen's feet. They both knew that Joan was right. Without saying a word, Maryellen slipped off the oxfords. Her summer sneakers had grass stains and holes in the toes, so she put on her last year's saddle shoes. The saddle shoes felt a bit tight, but they looked, as Carolyn said softly, "Perfect."

By using lots of bobby pins, Maryellen and Carolyn were able to wrangle Maryellen's still rather damp hair into a pretty good ponytail tied with a scarf.

Carolyn went off to the bathroom, and Maryellen checked herself against her hairdo sketches and the photos of her favorite movie star, Debbie Reynolds.

Hmph, Maryellen thought. She spotted a problem. Debbie Reynolds and most of the girls in Maryellen's sketches had bangs. Movie stars and models who wore poodle skirts always had bangs. Even Mamie Eisenhower, President Eisenhower's wife, wore bangs. Maryellen squinted at herself. She wanted so much to look *right* when everyone looked at her. She wanted to look *exactly* like Debbie Reynolds.

✳ The One and Only ✳

Well, how hard could it be to cut bangs? Maryellen asked herself. It was easy enough to *draw* them. Quick as a wink, she undid her ponytail, got scissors out of the desk, and *snip, snip, snip,* cut her hair in a line across her forehead.

Hmm, thought Maryellen as she looked in the mirror. For some reason, her bangs did not go straight across her forehead, like Debbie Reynolds's and Mamie Eisenhower's. Instead, her bangs slanted diagonally. They were longer on one side and shorter on the other. Maryellen immediately cut the longer side to make it match, and then looked in the mirror again. Now her bangs looked sort of zigzaggy.

She was trimming the ends to even them up when Carolyn returned from the bathroom and gasped, "STOP!"

Joan sat bolt upright in bed. "Oh, my gosh, Ellie. What've you done to yourself? You look like you got chopped by hedge clippers!"

Beverly opened her eyes. "Your hair's as short as Scooter's," said murmured sleepily.

"It is *not*," said Maryellen huffily. She tried to sound firm. She didn't want to let on that, now that she really

looked at her bangs, she was surprised—*horrified*, actually—by what she had done. It had happened so fast!
Just *snip, snip, snip*, and now . . . DISASTER! The bangs
stuck straight out from her forehead the way a tutu stuck
out from a ballerina's hips. And they were spiky, too.

I look like I have toothbrush bristles attached to my head,
thought Maryellen miserably. Oh, how she wished she
could tape her hair back on!

To hide her nearly teary face from her sisters,
Maryellen put the scissors down and gathered up the
snippets of hair from the floor. Her voice was only a little bit wavery when she said, "I think they look okay."

"They're much too short," said Joan, stating the
obvious.

"Never mind," said Carolyn kindly as she helped
Maryellen put the rest of her hair in a ponytail again.
"Your bangs will grow out fast."

Maryellen grimaced. She knew that Carolyn meant
to be soothing, but saying that her bangs would grow
out fast was hardly a compliment about how the bangs
looked right *now*.

"Wait till Mom sees you," said Joan. "She'll have a fit."

Now Maryellen was upset *and* worried. She tugged

at her bangs as if she could make them longer by pull-ing on them. She smoothed them and pushed them down to make them lie flat, but it was no use. As soon as she took her hand off them, her bangs sprang up and stuck straight out over her forehead like a sailor's salute.

"Maybe you could wear a scarf," said Carolyn thoughtfully. "You could wear it pulled low over your forehead, like a bandanna."

"And look like a pirate!" scoffed Joan.

"You could borrow my baseball cap," suggested Beverly.

"And look nutty as a fruitcake!" said Joan.

"Joan, will you cut it out?" said Carolyn. "You're making Ellie feel bad. How would you like to start the first day of school with a terrible haircut?"

"Ohhh," Maryellen moaned, feeling worse and worse. Now she wasn't going to be noticed because she was the one-and-only girl in the fourth grade who looked like a movie star. Instead, she was going to be stared at because she was the one-and-only girl with a crew cut.

"Girls!" Mom called from the kitchen. "Time for breakfast."

Maryellen took a deep, shuddery breath. *What is*

Mom going to say? she wondered, full of dread. She was grateful when Carolyn grabbed her hand as they walked together to the kitchen, followed by Scooter.

When Mom saw Maryellen, her jaw fell down and her eyebrows shot up. "Ellie," Mom gasped. "What on earth have you done?"

"I, well, I . . . " Maryellen faltered.

Mom held up her hand. "You don't need to tell me," she said. "I can see for myself. Bangs."

Tom, whose hair stuck straight out all over his head, said, "I *like* your bangs, Ellie."

"Bang!" yelled Mikey, banging his fist on his high-chair tray. "Bang, bang, bang!"

"*Ar-oof!*" barked Scooter, expressing his opinion, too.

"I'm sorry, Mom," said Maryellen over the cacophony. "Are you mad?"

"Well," said Mom. "I'm . . . *surprised*. But what's done is done and can't be undone. Besides, you're the one who has to wear the bangs, not me. But Ellie, honey, please talk to me first before you do any more do-it-yourself barbering."

"Oh, *Mom*," wailed Maryellen. She ran to Mom and threw her arms around her and hid her face against her. "Now I don't want to go to school at all!"

Mom hugged her, then pulled back and gently pressed Maryellen's bristly bangs down. Of course, they sprang right back up. "You've chosen a particularly, shall we say, *public* time to debut your bangs," Mom said. "But you're just going to have to face school, short bangs and all."

"And hey, your new skirt looks nice," said Dad cheerfully, trying to distract Maryellen from her misery. "It's a doozy!" He whistled his approval. "*Wheet, whee-oo!*"

"That's right. Just concentrate on your snazzy new skirt," Mom advised. "There's no question that, outfit-wise, you are going to be *the most* fashionable girl in the fourth grade. Right?"

Maryellen managed a watery grin. "I guess so."

"That's my girl," said Mom. "Now sit down and eat your breakfast. You don't want to feel *lightheaded* on your first day back."

"Mom!" Maryellen protested.

"Just kidding, just kidding," said Mom. She kissed Maryellen's exposed forehead. "Eat your cereal. Soon it'll be time to go."

✳ Unique ✳

Maryellen sat at the table, one hand pressed against her bangs, and the other holding a spoon, with which she only pretended to eat. Her stomach was tied in knots.

The knot tightened when the doorbell rang and Joan, who was wafting by the front door, called out, "Ellie, it's Davy, and he's got some other little boy with him."

"It's that mean boy, Wayne," Beverly hissed.

"Oh no!" Maryellen whispered. "*Wayne?*" Maryellen and Davy had planned to ride their bikes to school together, as they always did, but Davy hadn't said anything about including *Wayne*, of all people.

"I can't face them!" Maryellen said in a panic. "Please, somebody, tell them I'm not ready! Tell them I'm sick! Tell them I left already. Tell them *anything*. Just get them to go away."

Mom shook her head. "You're going to have to face people sooner or later," she said. "You might as well get it over with."

"I can't," Maryellen wailed. "Wayne is sure to say something smart-alecky."

"This is what happens when girls try to be friends with boys in fourth grade," said Joan. "It never works."

"*I'll* handle the boys," said Carolyn heroically.

Maryellen cowered in the breakfast nook while
Carolyn went straight to the front door and flung it
open. "Boys, Ellie told me to tell you that she doesn't
want to bike to school with you," Carolyn said firmly.
"She's afraid she'll get too sweaty, and she doesn't want
to ruin her outfit."

Maryellen heard Wayne snort and mutter, "Typical
girl!"

Davy just said, "Oh." He sounded disappointed
and confused. Maryellen didn't blame him, because
Carolyn's excuse did not ring true; Davy knew that
Maryellen wasn't the kind of girl who had *ever* worried
about getting messy in her entire life!

"You'd better get going, boys," Carolyn said in a no-
nonsense voice, "or you'll be late." Then, before she had
completely shut the door, Carolyn turned toward the
kitchen and called out, "The coast is clear, Ellie. I got
rid of the boys like you told me to!"

Maryellen groaned. All her hopes for looking great
on back-to-school day were ruined, cut off short like
her bangs. And now Davy was probably mad at her,
because Carolyn had made it sound like Maryellen
wanted him to get lost.

So far, this sure wasn't the wonderful start to a wonderful year in fourth grade that she had imagined. Maryellen wondered, *Could this morning get any worse?*

Tickled
Pink

A s she rode her bike to school, Maryellen tried to follow Mom's advice and forget about her hair and concentrate on her skirt. The skirt certainly was wonderful. It poufed out a bit, very gracefully, as she pedaled her bike. If *anything* could salvage this day, the black-and-pink poodle skirt could. She hoped that everyone would be so dazzled by her skirt that they wouldn't notice her hair.

When she got to the school playground, where the students were milling around before lining up to go into the school building, Maryellen parked her bike and looked for Davy so that she could apologize to him. Her heart sank when she saw that Davy was shooting baskets with Wayne. Nevertheless, she squared her shoulders and made herself march toward the boys.

"Hey, Ellie!" a voice shouted. "We're over here!"

Maryellen turned and saw Karen King waving wildly amid the throng of students. She waved back and ran to join Karen and Karen, thinking that really, it would be better to apologize to Davy later, when he was alone. Halfway to the Karens, Maryellen stopped short. She blinked. *Karen Stohlman was wearing a black-and-pink poodle skirt exactly like hers!*

"SURPRISE!" the Karens sang out. Karen Stohlman twirled, lifting her arms over her head like a ballerina. She was wearing a white blouse and saddle shoes, too.

"Look!" gushed Karen King. "Yesterday, Karen went out and got a poodle skirt just like yours."

"We're twins, Ellie," Karen Stohlman said gaily. "My mother and I went shopping at O'Neal's yesterday, and . . ." She stopped. "Gosh, Ellie—you cut your hair!"

"Whoa! I'll say!" said Karen King. "Bangs. Uh, *wow*. Aren't they kind of too short?"

"Yes," said Maryellen sharply. She turned to Karen Stohlman, eager to get off the subject. "So you got your skirt yesterday?"

"Yes!" said Karen Stohlman. "To match yours. Isn't this the best surprise ever?"

"Mm-hmm," said Maryellen. She smiled, because she knew the Karens expected her to smile. They expected her to be delighted—to be tickled pink!—and she herself thought she *should* be. But her smile was crooked and forced. She couldn't help noticing that Karen's ponytail was longer than hers, and of course, Karen didn't have ridiculous bristle bangs like her unfortunate ones. Furthermore, Karen's skirt was much fuller than her own. Carolyn's crinoline had been laundered so many times that it had lost some of its oomph, so Maryellen's poodle looked disappointingly limp next to Karen's.

In her heart of hearts, Maryellen had wanted to be unique. She had wanted to stand out as the one-and-only girl in the fourth grade who looked like a movie star. Now she couldn't. In fact, Karen looked more stylish and movie-star-ish than she did. *Karen Stohlman has stolen my idea,* Maryellen thought. *She's a copycat!*

"Patty Zender has the same skirt, too," said Karen King.

"You're kidding!" said Maryellen. For some reason, it made her feel a lot better to know about Patty Zender. *So I wouldn't have been the only one in a poodle skirt anyway,* she realized. *I wouldn't have been unique even if Karen Stohlman hadn't copied me.*

The idea of three matching poodle skirts on the playground cheered Maryellen up. *Well, we might as well make the best of it*, she thought as she waved Patty over to join them. "Come on, Karen," she said. "The three of us can pretend we're the McDoogal Sisters."

Maryellen held her hand up to her mouth as if it was a microphone and she was on TV. "Ladies and gentlemen," she announced. "We're everyone's favorite trio, the McDoogal Sisters, and we're going to sing for you our big hit of 1954, 'Time to Go.'"

Karen Stohlman and Patty giggled, but they sang along with Maryellen, "Time to go, oh, it's time to go . . . " They copied Maryellen and put their hands on their hips and swayed from side to side. When Karen King sang the "doot-dootle-doot-doots" in the background, they twirled around and made their skirts flare out, and at the end of the song, they sank down in curtsies, all at the same time.

It turned out to be quite fun to be part of the poodle-skirt trio. Singing and dancing helped Maryellen forget about her terrible bangs and the misunderstanding with

Davy. She tucked her disappointment and her annoyance at Karen Stohlman away, deep down in a hidden corner of her heart, and sang—almost—as if she truly *were* tickled pink.

Pretty soon, the school bell clanged and it really was "time to go," or at least time to line up, boys in one line, girls in another. The two Karens, Patty, and Maryellen went upstairs to Mrs. Humphrey's fourth-grade classroom together, feeling grown-up and superior to the third-graders, who were still on the first floor with the other lower grades.

Maryellen's saddle shoes squeezed her toes uncomfortably and went *tsk-tsk-tsk* as she climbed the stairs. It was as if they were scolding her for making the mistake of wearing them even though they were definitely too small.

"Welcome, fourth-graders!" said Mrs. Humphrey as the students entered the room. "Please be seated. Take any desk."

Maryellen sank gratefully into a seat and banged her heels softly on the floor to make space for her toes inside her shoes. The felt poodle skirt was actually too hot for this sunny September morning, and Carolyn's crinoline itched under her armpits. She wriggled and scratched as inconspicuously as she could.

"Fleas, pardner?" Davy asked sympathetically, from his temporary seat behind her. "On loan from Scooter?"

Maryellen knew that Davy was only joking with her in a friendly way. Even so, she felt a tiny prick of annoyance.

And then Wayne, next to Davy, snickered. "Ooh, ooh! Ah, ah!" Wayne chirruped like a monkey.

When Maryellen turned around to face the boys, Wayne was scratching his head and his armpits, pretending to be a monkey scratching its fleas. Suddenly, he stopped mid-scratch and stared. "Yikes!" he said. "What happened to *you*, Baldy?" He put his hand flat on top of his head and wiggled his stiff fingers over his forehead.

"Holy cow," breathed Davy, his eyes wide at the sight of Maryellen's sticky-out bangs.

"Hmph!" snorted Maryellen, turning away to hide how hurt she was. She had expected teasing from Wayne, but not from *Davy*. Up till now, Davy had always made her feel better about things, not worse. She decided that she wasn't going to apologize to him for what Carolyn had done. So there!

Maryellen turned her attention to Mrs. Humphrey, who was pleasantly plump and good-natured looking, and who smiled and nodded at the students as they entered. After everyone was seated, Mrs. Humphrey said, "Now that we're all here, I'll call the roll and assign permanent seats alphabetically."

Since Maryellen's last name began with L, which was right in the middle of the alphabet, she knew that she had a little time to look around. She was glad to see lots of maps in the classroom, rolled up like window shades above the blackboard, because she loved thinking about other countries and far-off places and different languages. She was not so glad to see, above the blackboard, green placards with models of uppercase and lowercase letters in white script swooping along white handwriting lines. Handwriting was not her best subject. She recognized all of the kids except one new girl, who had long, dark braids and, Maryellen saw with amazement, *pierced ears*! Talk about grown-up!

"Larkin, Maryellen?" Mrs. Humphrey called.

"Present," said Maryellen. She stood up, keeping

her arms tightly close to her sides so that Carolyn's crinoline wouldn't slip.

Mrs. Humphrey beamed at Maryellen and looked very pleased as she pointed to the desk she wanted her to take. "I could have guessed that you were a Larkin," she said. "You and your sisters Joan and Carolyn are as alike as three peas in a pod. I'd recognize that Larkin nose anywhere. I had your sister Carolyn in my class a few years ago and Joan a few years before that. They were excellent students."

"Yes, Mrs. Humphrey," said Maryellen, thinking, *I'm off to a good start. Mrs. Humphrey likes me already!* She slid into the chair at her assigned desk, which was behind Jimmy Lansing, as usual. After three years behind Jimmy Lansing, she was getting to know the spindly back of *his* neck very well.

"I'll bet you're as tidy and organized as Carolyn and Joan were, too," said Mrs. Humphrey.

Maryellen's smile faded a bit. *Uh-oh,* she thought. Mrs. Humphrey would soon figure out that she was not tidy or organized. Then again, Mrs. Humphrey would also soon figure out that she wasn't Carolyn or Joan.

The funny thing was, Mrs. Humphrey *didn't* seem to figure that out. As the morning progressed, pretty soon everyone in the class knew that when Mrs. Humphrey said "Carolyn," she meant "Maryellen." It was confusing. During math class, whenever Mrs. Humphrey said, "Tell us how to divide these numbers, Care—" Karen King, Karen Stohlman, and Carol Turner all looked up, expecting to be called on. After a while, Maryellen looked up, too, because often Mrs. Humphrey was looking straight at her and calling her Carolyn. If that happened and Maryellen didn't look up, Wayne took it upon himself to lean across the aisle and poke her hard in the ribs and hiss, "She means *you*."

To add to the confusion, when Mrs. Humphrey said "Joan," everyone including Maryellen naturally thought she was calling on Joan Martin, who sat right behind Maryellen. But sometimes Mrs. Humphrey was looking at Maryellen and calling *her* Joan. When that happened, both Maryellen and Joan Martin would answer Mrs. Humphrey at the same time.

Maryellen couldn't help noticing that Mrs. Humphrey was starting to get flustered and looking annoyed every time she called her by the wrong name, whether she responded or not. It was almost as if Mrs. Humphrey suspected Maryellen of trying to trick her deliberately.

This is what happens, thought Maryellen, *when even your teacher is a hand-me-down from your sisters.*

✳

At lunch, Karen King said to Maryellen, "Mrs. Humphrey seems to think that your name is 'Carolyn-Joan-I-mean-Maryellen.'"

Maryellen grinned. Quickly, she drew a sketch on her napkin of a frowning Mrs. Humphrey saying, "Carolyn! Joan! Maryellen! Whoever!" and pointing her finger like Uncle Sam in a recruitment poster. Under the drawing, she wrote in capital letters: THIS MEANS YOU!

All the girls giggled. Davy, who was passing their table, asked, "What's so funny?"

Wayne, who was right behind Davy, snatched the napkin out of Maryellen's hands. "Get a load of this," he crowed. "A cartoon of Mrs. Humphrey!"

"Give it back!" Maryellen demanded, twisting in her seat.

But Wayne waved the napkin over Maryellen's head, just out of her reach. "You can't make me," he taunted.

"Got it!" shouted Davy, snatching the napkin out of Wayne's hands.

Just then, someone took the napkin out of Davy's hand. "Hey!" he began to protest, until he saw that it was Mrs. Humphrey.

"Uh-oh," breathed Karen King.

"I am disappointed in you children," said Mrs. Humphrey. "Fighting over a napkin! Is this the proper way for fourth-graders to behave in the lunchroom?"

"No, Mrs. Humphrey," said Davy, Maryellen, and the two Karens. Wayne had somehow disappeared, slithering away in the lunchroom crowd like a snake.

Maryellen got very red in the face while Mrs. Humphrey looked at the drawing on the napkin. "I'm sorry, Mrs. Humphrey," she began.

"Why, I'm surprised at you, Care-Jo-no-oh! Miss Larkin," interrupted Mrs. Humphrey. She held the napkin with the very tips of her fingers as if it were radio-active, tore the napkin in half, dropped the two pieces in the trash, and left.

"Davy! Look what you did," said Maryellen crossly.

"What do you mean?" asked Davy. "I took the napkin away from Wayne to give it back to you."

"Well, if you hadn't been yelling and waving it around, Mrs. Humphrey wouldn't have noticed it," said Maryellen. "You got me into trouble."

"You got yourself into trouble," said Davy, "by drawing the cartoon in the first place."

"I—" Maryellen started to say.

"Never mind!" said Davy. "I'll get lost. That's what you want me to do, right? Just like this morning." He turned on his heel and stormed off.

"Yikes," said Karen King softly. "He's mad."

"Well, I'm mad, too," said Maryellen. "Now Mrs. Humphrey doesn't like me, and it's Davy's fault."

"I told you boys were pains," said Karen Stohlman.

"I think it's Wayne who's the pain," said Karen King. "He's stuck himself onto Davy like glue."

"Well, Davy should unstick himself," said Maryellen crossly. "Why does he put up with Wayne, anyway? I don't like him."

"And I don't think Mrs. Humphrey liked your cartoon, Ellie," said Karen King, who prided herself on telling the truth no matter how unpleasant it might be.

"I never meant for her to see it," said Maryellen miserably. "She may not be sure who I am, but now she *is* sure that she doesn't like me."

"Well, we still like you, Care-Jo-no-oh! Miss Larkin," said Karen King kindly.

"Thanks," said Maryellen. Her smile was weak but grateful. What would she ever do without the Karens, her two best, best friends, especially *now*, when for the first time ever, she and Davy were on the outs?

✳

That afternoon, when Maryellen was back at home changing into her play clothes, Joan asked, "So how was the first day of fourth grade?"

"Fine," sighed Maryellen, sounding as if she meant the opposite.

"Mrs. Humphrey is nice, isn't she?" said Carolyn.

"I guess so," said Maryellen gloomily. She patted Scooter in a distracted way.

"You don't sound very enthusiastic," said Joan. "What happened?"

"Mrs. Humphrey kept calling me Joan or Carolyn,"

Maryellen grumbled, "and I, well, I drew a cartoon about it and she saw it."

"Uh-oh," said Carolyn.

"I didn't mean to be disrespectful," said Maryellen. "Really I didn't. I was just sort of making a joke about how she didn't seem to know that I was me."

"Did you tell Mrs. Humphrey that you were sorry?" asked Joan.

"Yes," said Maryellen. "And I really am sorry."

"Mrs. Humphrey will forgive you," said Joan. "She knows that it's what you do *after* you've made a mistake that matters. Anyway, *everyone* makes mistakes."

"Yes!" Carolyn interjected brightly. "Like your bangs!"

"Ohh," moaned Maryellen, not at all cheered up. "Mrs. Humphrey never would have seen the cartoon if Wayne hadn't snatched it and Davy hadn't waved it around."

"What did I tell you?" said Joan. "You cannot be friends with boys in the fourth grade. They're—"

"Pains?" suggested Maryellen, remembering what Karen Stohlman had said about her brother.

"Yes, for a while," said Joan. "They're okay again in

high school." Maryellen knew that, of course, Joan was thinking of dreamy Jerry, to whom she was practically engaged. "But right now, Ellie-mellie, if you're smart, you'll concentrate on your friendship with the Karens."

"Right," said Carolyn. "Girls won't let you down."

Maryellen hoped that Carolyn was right—and that Joan was wrong. She really didn't want to have to wait until high school to be friends with Davy again. In her heart of hearts, she was sorry about their fight, and she already missed him.

The Lunch Bunch

✳ CHAPTER EIGHT ✳

he next morning, Maryellen put on the plaid school dress and the brown oxfords that she had inherited from Carolyn. She waited, but Davy did not stop by to bike to school with her, so she rode to school by herself.

It was amazing, thought Maryellen as Mrs. Humphrey explained long division, how much better her brain worked when her feet weren't squashed and she didn't have to worry all the time about Carolyn's crinoline falling down.

When the math lesson was finished, Mrs. Humphrey pulled down the map of the world.

Good, thought Maryellen. She liked geography. She always helped Dad plot their route and navigate the map when they went on car trips, and she liked to doodle the shapes of different states and countries just for fun.

✻ The One and Only ✻

"Boys and girls," said Mrs. Humphrey importantly, "in fourth grade, we study history, social studies, and current events. To understand any of those subjects, we need to know geography. In fact, geography is so important that we're going to have a class Geography Bee at the end of every month, and the winners will get prizes."

The class murmured with excitement. Maryellen and the Karens exchanged delighted glances, and Maryellen saw Wayne playfully punch Davy in the arm. Everybody loved bees and prizes!

Mrs. Humphrey covered the name of one of the countries on the map of Europe. "Now," she said, "who can tell me the name of this country?"

Maryellen shot her hand up. She knew that the country was Italy, because she knew that Italy was shaped like a boot.

Mrs. Humphrey glanced at Maryellen, but she called on the new girl with the long braids and earrings, even though the girl had not raised her hand. "Angela?" Mrs. Humphrey said.

The new girl smiled, and her whole face lit up as if the sun was shining on it. *"Italia,"* she said.

"Yes, good," said Mrs. Humphrey. "This is the country your family came from. In English, we call it *Italy*."

The class murmured again. Everyone stared at the new girl, who stopped smiling and looked down at her desk.

Oh, so the new girl is **Italian**, thought Maryellen.

Mrs. Humphrey covered the name of another country on the map. She had not even asked for its name before almost every hand in the room went up.

"That's Germany," Davy called out. "Everybody knows that, because the Germans were our enemies in World War Two."

"Japan and Italy were against us, too," added Karen Stohlman with a sideways glance at the new girl. Maryellen hoped Angela did not understand enough English to be offended. Karen Stohlman went on, "My uncle fought in Italy. He was a hero, but the Italians—"

"Yes, well, the war ended in 1945, nearly ten years ago," Mrs. Humphrey interrupted briskly. "The Germans, Italians, and Japanese are not our enemies anymore. Let's move right along, now. Who can tell me the name of the capital of Germany?"

This time only Maryellen's hand went up.

"Uh, yes?" said Mrs. Humphrey, who seemed to have decided not to call Maryellen by any name at all, much to the relief of everyone in the class.

"The capital of Germany is Berlin," said Maryellen. She knew all about Berlin because her sister Joan had written a report about it last year, and Maryellen had drawn the maps for her, since she was so good at sketching. "After the war, Berlin was divided up. The Russians have one part, and now their part is behind the Iron Curtain."

"The Russians have a curtain made of *iron*?" asked Wayne, sounding skeptical.

"It isn't real," said Maryellen. "But the Russians won't let people come and go freely and they keep things secret on their side, so it's as if they've closed a curtain. America doesn't like the way the Russians are treating people, so now the Russians are sort of our enemies and we're in something called a Cold War with them."

"What's a cold war?" Patty Zender asked.

"It means that each side tries to have more bombs than the other side, even though they don't use them," said Maryellen. "We're not fighting battles against the Russians, but we don't trust them and we're not friendly with them, either."

Mrs. Humphrey smiled at Maryellen. "Good explanation," she said. "Splendid."

Maryellen beamed. Maybe Mrs. Humphrey would forgive her for the napkin cartoon and like her again. She was sorry when geography was over and Mrs. Humphrey handed out handwriting workbooks.

Last year, in third grade, all of her classmates had been excited about learning to write in script instead of printing. But Maryellen had discovered that because she was left-handed, her letters seemed to lean in the wrong direction, tilting and wobbling so badly that no one could read them, not even her grandparents, to whom she wrote practically every week. Finally, Maryellen had solved the problem by inventing a sort of fake script for herself, which she made by smooshing printed letters together. She tried hard now, she really did, to make her loopy letters look nice and neat. But the handwriting book got in her way, and no matter how careful she was, she smudged the words she had written when her left hand passed over them.

Mrs. Humphrey came by and looked at Maryellen's book over her shoulder. She didn't say anything, but Maryellen knew that her workbook page looked messy.

When it was time to line up for lunch, Mrs. Humphrey announced, "Boys and girls, I sometimes invite students to join what I call my 'Lunch Bunch' and meet me here in the classroom after lunch instead of going out for recess. Today, I'm inviting Angela, Davy, and, uh . . ." Mrs. Humphrey paused to be sure she got the name right, then said, "*Maryellen* to join me."

Karen King rolled her eyes at Maryellen. Mrs. Humphrey had made her announcement in a cheery tone of voice, as if joining the Lunch Bunch was a privilege. But everyone knew perfectly well that it wasn't.

"It isn't much of a 'bunch' anyway," Karen Stohlman said while the girls ate their sandwiches in the cafeteria. "It's just you, that new Italian girl who doesn't speak any English, and Davy, who needs help with multiplication."

"Gosh, Ellie," said Karen King. "Do you think Mrs. Humphrey is punishing you because of that cartoon?"

"No," sighed Maryellen. "I think I'm in the Lunch

Bunch because Mrs. Humphrey doesn't like my script handwriting."

Maryellen's Lunch Bunch hunch turned out to be right.

When she went back to the classroom, Davy didn't even look up from his math book.

Mrs. Humphrey said, "Now, Care—uh, Maryellen, let's talk about your handwriting. I see that you're not really writing in cursive. You're just running your printed letters together. Is that what your teacher showed you how to do in third grade?"

"No," admitted Maryellen. "I kind of invented my handwriting all by myself."

"I see," said Mrs. Humphrey. "Well, you are in the fourth grade now, and I think that your script should look like everyone else's. With practice, I am sure that your script can look like those beautiful letters on the placards there, above the blackboard. Will you try?"

"Yes," promised Maryellen earnestly.

"Good!" said Mrs. Humphrey. "I've thought of a way that you can practice your handwriting and help Angela learn English at the same time." Mrs. Humphrey handed Maryellen a composition book.

"Now, we both know that you are quite good at simple line drawings, like *cartoons*, don't we?" said Mrs.
Humphrey.

Maryellen looked up sharply. Was Mrs. Humphrey
still mad about the napkin cartoon?

But Mrs. Humphrey had a twinkle in her eye. "So,
I was thinking that you could draw objects and write
their names in English for Angela. Use your best handwriting, because you will be making a dictionary for
Angela. You can begin with objects in the classroom."

"Yes, ma'am!" said Maryellen, feeling hopeful that
she was forgiven. Mrs. Humphrey's plan sounded sort
of fun. Well, except for the handwriting part.

For the rest of the week, the Lunch Bunch met every
day after lunch in the classroom. Davy did not speak to
Maryellen, and she did not speak to him. It made her
sad, because by now, she had fully admitted to herself
that Davy was right; she had gotten herself into trouble
by drawing the cartoon. She also admitted to herself
that she had gotten mad at Davy because she resented
how he seemed to prefer being with Wayne. But even
when he wasn't working on his multiplication tables
with Mrs. Humphrey, Davy ignored her.

It was fun to work with Angela, though. The two girls went around the classroom, and Angela would point to an object, such as a window.

"Window," Maryellen would say in English.

"Window," Angela would repeat. Then Maryellen would sketch the window in the composition book and label it in painstaking cursive, and Angela would read the name aloud.

Pretty soon, Angela began to teach Maryellen the names of the objects in Italian. Maryellen loved the Italian words because they sounded so pretty, and they were fun to pronounce because they were tickly and delicious in her mouth. Window was *finestra*, desk was *banco,* and book was *libro.* She felt almost as if she were singing when she pronounced the Italian words that Angela taught her.

Mrs. Humphrey let Maryellen and Angela pull down the maps, and they taught each other the names of the seven continents, which were easy, and then the names of the big countries like India and China, and then the names of the tricky little countries that made up Europe. Maryellen could never stump Angela at any of the European countries. Even when she just sketched their outlines in the composition book, Angela could name them quick as a wink in both English and Italian.

When the girls ran out of objects in the classroom to name, Maryellen drew a person waving and saying hi. Then she waved to Angela and said, "Hi!"

"Hi!" repeated Angela. "In Italian, *ciao*."

"*Chow*," repeated Maryellen. "Thanks!"

"In Italian, *grazie*," said Angela. She pointed to herself and then to Maryellen and said, "In Italian, *amiche*. In English, I think, *friends*?"

"Oh, yes," said Maryellen. "Absolutely friends."

"Good!" said Angela, smiling her sunshiny smile.

After that, Maryellen taught Angela how to count to a hundred in English and Angela taught her how to count to *cento* in Italian. It was all unexpectedly fun. The only slightly worrisome thing was that her handwriting was not really improving. Angela never complained, but Maryellen could see that Angela had a hard time reading her cursive unless she went back to her old looped-and-linked style.

One day at lunchtime, Angela gave Maryellen a gift. It was a pretty plastic headband.

"Thanks, Angela!" said Maryellen. "It's pretty."

"Come," said Angela. She led Maryellen to the mirror by the classroom sink, and showed her how to use the headband to push her bangs back from her forehead and sort of hide them under the headband.

"Oh!" said Maryellen, delighted. "*Grazie*, Angela! *Grazie* very much!" Impulsively, she gave Angela a hug. "You're the first person who has actually come up with a helpful solution to the problem of my bangs!"

Angela smiled and hugged Maryellen back.

Another day Karen King was absent and Karen Stohlman had ballet, so Maryellen walked her bike home with Angela, who lived near the school.

"Come in?" Angela asked.

Maryellen felt a little bit shy at first, but the minute they walked in the door, Angela's dog trotted up to welcome them and wagged his tail hello.

"Oh!" Maryellen exclaimed, kneeling to pet the dog. "What's his name?"

"Amerigo," said Angela.

"Oh, he's so cute!" said Maryellen. "My dog is named Scooter. Hi, Amerigo! I mean, *ciao*."

Angela's mother and father were at work, but her grandmother, whom Angela introduced as "Nonna," was in the kitchen making meatballs. Maryellen had never seen anyone making meatballs before. At her house, spaghetti and meatballs came straight out of the Chef Boy-Ar-Dee can. After the girls washed their hands, Nonna let them make meatballs, too.

"This is fun," said Maryellen, rolling the meat in her palms.

"Like making snowballs," said Angela.

"Oh, did you have snow where you lived in Italy?" asked Maryellen enviously.

Angela nodded yes.

"I've always wanted to see snow," said Maryellen. "It almost never happens here in Florida. Anyway, I've never seen it snow."

Nonna let Angela give a meatball to Amerigo, and he leapt up into the air to take it from her hand. Maryellen clapped and cheered. "I'd love to teach Scooter to do that," she said.

Maryellen was sorry when it was time to go. As she was leaving, Nonna said something to her in rapid Italian. Angela laughed and translated it. "Nonna says, next time, stay for dinner, have meatballs. But no jumping for meatballs like Amerigo!"

✳ The Lunch Bunch ✳

"*Grazie*, Nonna!" said Maryellen happily. She grinned and hopped a little hop, to show Nonna that she understood.

✳

At the end of that week, on Friday, Maryellen wore her poodle skirt to school again. Her bangs weren't bothering her anymore, thanks to the headband from Angela, and she did love the skirt, even if she was not the one-and-only girl who had one.

Later that day, as she and the Karens were leaving school to walk home, Karen Stohlman said, "Next time you're going to wear your poodle skirt, call me first and I'll wear mine, too, so we can be twins."

Maryellen winced an invisible wince, but she said, "We can call Patty, too, and be the McDoogal Sisters on the playground again."

"Except you're never *on* the playground anymore," said Karen King. "Not after lunch, anyway. How long are you going to be in that Lunch Bunch? All year?"

"I don't know," said Maryellen. "I don't mind it, really. It's sort of fun. Like today, Angela pointed to my skirt and taught me to say *barboncino francese*, which is

'French poodle' in Italian. Don't you love that? Angela loves dogs. She has one—not a poodle, but a spaniel, named Amerigo—and he's adorable! Angela says—"

"Wait," Karen Stohlman interrupted sharply. "You've met Angela's dog?"

"Yes," said Maryellen, "when I went to her house."

"You went to Angela's house?" asked Karen King.

"Yes," said Maryellen, "but what I'm trying to say is that Angela told me that in Italian, dogs go *arf arf* instead of *woof woof* like they do in English. Isn't that funny?"

"Angela this and Angela that," said Karen Stohlman. Her voice sounded a little brittle. "You've met her dog and you've been to her house. You're getting awfully chummy with her."

"She's nice," said Maryellen. "You'd like her, too, if you got to know her."

The two Karens exchanged a look.

"I don't think so," said Karen King.

"What do you mean?" asked Maryellen.

"She's so different," said Karen Stohlman. "She has those long braids, and *pierced ears*. She stands out like a sore thumb."

✳ The Lunch Bunch ✳

"I think the ways she's different make her interesting," said Maryellen. "And what's wrong with standing out, anyway?"

"Well," said Karen King, as if she were stating the obvious, "no one wants to stand out for a weird reason."

"Right," said Karen Stohlman. "I mean, do you like standing out and being different because of your polio?"

Maryellen was speechless. It had never occurred to her before that her friends thought her polio made her *weird*. When she recovered from her shock and hurt, she said curtly, "I *did* want to stand out by being the only girl who had a poodle skirt, but you copied me."

Now Karen Stohlman was surprised. "I thought you would like it if we matched!" she exclaimed. "I didn't realize you were so set on being 'different' and 'interesting.' No wonder you like Angela so much; she's different all right. For Pete's sake, she's *Italian*."

"What's wrong with that?" asked Maryellen. "So what?"

"So, Italy was friends with Germany and Japan during the war," said Karen King. "The Italians were our *enemies*."

"But that was nearly ten years ago!" said Maryellen. "Remember how Mrs. Humphrey said that we're not enemies anymore? And anyway, Angela is just Angela. She's not responsible for Italy during the war. She wasn't even born yet."

"Fine," said Karen Stohlman with a shrug. "Go ahead and be disloyal if that's what you want to do."

"Disloyal?" said Maryellen.

"Yes," said Karen Stohlman tartly. "You seem to have forgotten, Ellie, but Italians killed my uncle during the war. I could never be friends with an Italian."

"But—" Maryellen sputtered.

Karen Stohlman talked over her. "And I could never be friends with anyone who was *friends* with an Italian."

"Me neither," said Karen King.

Maryellen felt as if she had been walloped in the stomach. Her two best friends—the only old friends she had *left* now without Davy—seemed to be saying that they would not be friends with her anymore if she was friends with Angela. For a moment, she felt flummoxed, unsure what to do. Then an unexpected feeling surprised her, a spurt of red-hot anger. *How dare they*

* The Lunch Bunch *

tell me how to act?

"Well," Maryellen said quietly. "I can't be friends with anyone who couldn't be friends with someone who was friends with an Italian."

"Then I guess—I guess that means we can't be friends anymore?" squeaked Karen Stohlman.

"Yeah, I guess it does," said Maryellen.

"Come on, Karen," said Karen Stohlman. "Let's go."

Maryellen watched the two Karens walk away. She felt very lonely standing there on the sidewalk all by herself.

Then Karen Stohlman turned around and called, "And *I* don't have any Italian *bar-bon-chee-noh fran-cheh-seh* on *my* skirt. I have a regular American French poodle!"

The two Karens ran away, so Maryellen wasn't sure whether Karen Stohlman heard her shout, "You wouldn't have any poodle *at all* if you weren't a copycat!"

Maryellen's Cold War

✷ CHAPTER NINE ✷

 ake new friends
But kee-eep thee-ee old;
One is silver
And the other's gold.

It was Wednesday, two weeks later, and Maryellen's Girl Scout troop was meeting in the cafeteria after school for the first time. At their last meeting back in June, at the end of third grade, the troop had held its Flying Up ceremony and the girls had flown up from Brownies to Girl Scouts. So this was their first time wearing their green uniforms, green socks, and berets instead of brown dresses, brown socks, and beanies.

Maryellen sighed. Angela was not a Girl Scout, so she was alone. She thought about how she and the two

Karens had really looked forward to being Girl Scouts together, and how just before school began, they'd talked about earning badges, selling cookies, and going on overnight camping trips. Now, as they sang "Make New Friends," Maryellen couldn't even look the two Karens in the eye. The three of them sure had not "kept the old," friendship-wise. The Karens obviously didn't think that *she* was gold.

When Mrs. Nichols, their troop leader, told the girls to choose groups of four to share tents on their first overnight campout, which was to take place in October, the two Karens rushed to invite Patty Zender and Carol Turner to share the tent with them. That meant that Maryellen would have to be in the leftovers tent with Mrs. Nichols and her daughter Debbie, who wasn't even *in* the troop because she was too young.

Maryellen sighed again as she watched the Karens, Patty, and Carol giggling over the Caper Chart. They had all signed up for KP, which was kitchen patrol and the most fun job on the Caper Chart because you were in charge of finding sticks for roasting hot dogs and for toasting marshmallows for s'mores. Later, during the meeting, Maryellen saw that the Karens had used matching material to make their sit-upons. *And I just know they'll sit upon their sit-upons far away from me*, she thought.

It had been this way for two weeks now, ever since the conversation about Angela.

"It's as if the three of us are having our own little private Cold War," Maryellen said later to Carolyn on Wednesday night as they got ready for bed. "We don't fight. They just snub Angela and me, and they try to get other kids to ignore us, too. Of course, Davy *already* acts as if I don't exist."

"It's like you're blacklisted," said Carolyn, stepping over Scooter, who was in the way as usual. "We learned about blacklisting in social studies. It means that you're excluded because people don't like something you did or something you believe."

"Exactly!" said Maryellen. "The Karens don't talk to Angela and me on the playground before school. They won't sit at a lunch table with Angela and me or walk home after school with us. It's like the Karens and I are on different sides of the Iron Curtain—as if we're enemies, when we used to be friends and allies."

"But do you *want* to be friends with them after what

they said about Angela?" asked Carolyn.

"Oh, I don't know," said Maryellen. "They hurt my feelings, and I think they're completely wrong about Angela. I mean, Angela's just a kid—she didn't have anything to do with the war, which ended a long time ago, before Angela was born."

"Lots of people are still mad about the war, though, Ellie," Carolyn pointed out. "Even Mom and Dad don't like us to buy things like purses or hair clips that are made in Japan."

"But Angela is a *person*," said Maryellen, pulling on her pajamas. "You can't just lump her together with a gigantic group of people and then cross her off because she's part of that group. The Karens would like her if they got to know her the way I did. Still," she admitted, "I miss Karen and Karen, just like I miss Davy. And remember what Joan said about how it's what you do *after* a mistake that matters? The Karens are making a mistake about Angela, but if they stopped their mistake, I'd be glad to be friends again."

"The Karens *have* been your friends for a long time," Carolyn agreed. "But you're doing the right thing, sticking up for Angela, even though it's hard.

I know that's probably cold comfort."

"Well," sighed Maryellen, "maybe cold comfort is all you get in a Cold War."

✳

"Fourth-graders!" said Mrs. Humphrey in her most listen-because-this-is-important voice. "Today is the day for our Geography Bee."

"Hurray!" the class cheered.

"Count off by twos," said Mrs. Humphrey. "Then all of you on Team One stand by the windows, and all of you on Team Two stand by the door. Wayne, there is no reason for you to be talking right now."

In a jiffy, the class was divided into two teams. Maryellen was glad to see that Angela was on Team Two, too, as she was. She was not as pleased to see that both Karens were also on Team Two, as was Davy.

Everyone was so fizzy with excitement that Mrs. Humphrey had to clap her hands. "I'd like your full attention, please," she said. When everyone had quieted down, Mrs. Humphrey went on. "Now, I will ask each one of you a geography question, and you must answer with the name of a country. If you answer incorrectly, you must take your seat. The team with the last person standing wins the Geography Bee, and all members of the winning team will receive prizes."

"What are the prizes?" asked Wayne.

"You'll see," said Mrs. Humphrey, sounding merrily mysterious.

"Can we help each other?" asked Patty Zender.

"Yes," said Mrs. Humphrey. "Even after you're sitting down, you can help a teammate. You may not tell your teammate the answer to any question, but you may act out a clue silently, as if you are playing the game Charades."

The class murmured and giggled. The Bee sounded like so much fun!

"All right, let's begin," said Mrs. Humphrey. "Ready?"

"Yes!" cheered the class.

Maryellen's heart rose when she saw that Mrs. Humphrey had made maps just like the ones that she had made for Angela. Mrs. Humphrey had drawn the outlines of different countries but had not labeled them. Both Team One and Team Two had no trouble naming the continents like Africa and Australia. They did well naming the big countries like India and China, too. But when Mrs. Humphrey started to ask for the names of the smaller countries that made up Europe and the quirky-shaped ones that made up South America, both Ones and Twos started dropping like flies.

Pretty soon, there were three students left on Team One: Joan Martin, Carol Turner, and Jimmy Lansing. The only Team Twos left were Karen Stohlman, Angela, and Maryellen. Then Maryellen said Argentina by mistake when she should have said Chile, so she had to sit down. Joan Martin missed Chile, too, but Angela got it. Jimmy Lansing missed on Bolivia, and so did Angela, but Carol got it.

"All right, girls," said Mrs. Humphrey to Carol and Karen Stohlman. "It is down to the two of you." She held up the outline of a country. "Carol?" she asked.

"Spain?" said Carol.

"No, I'm sorry," said Mrs. Humphrey. She turned to Karen Stohlman. "Karen, if you can name this country correctly, your team, Team Two, will win the Geography Bee. If you cannot name it correctly, then you and Carol will keep going until one of you can name a country that the other one cannot name."

France, it's France! Maryellen wanted to shout out to Karen Stohlman, who was biting her lip and looking as if she was not sure of the correct answer. *Oh, how can I help her?* Maryellen fretted. Then she had a brilliant idea. She waved to Karen Stohlman to get her attention. Karen looked at her with an expression that was wary but desperate. Maryellen stood up and made the shape of a full skirt around herself. She made Patty Zender stand up, and pointed to the skirt of her dress. Then she pointed to the skirt of Karen's dress, too.

Karen looked befuddled.

Suddenly, Davy jumped up. He put his hands on his hips and swayed from side to side, singing silently. The class howled with delighted hilarious laughter. Davy twirled, and then he sank down in a deep curtsy.

Karen looked even more at a loss than before.

Then Angela held her fists by her chin like paws and mimed barking like a dog.

"Skirts and singing and a dog?" said Karen, frowning. "Oh!" she exclaimed, rising up on her toes. "I get it! You mean our *poodle* skirts."

Angela nodded vigorously. Davy pretended to collapse in relief. Maryellen put one hand in front of the other, making the sign from Charades that meant *the word that goes before.*

"Oh!" Karen exclaimed again. "They're French poodles. So—" She turned to Mrs. Humphrey. "That country must be France!"

"Yes!" said Mrs. Humphrey. "Team Two wins the Geography Bee. Congratulations!"

"HURRAY!" shouted the students on Team Two, jumping out of their seats. Karen Stohlman ran over and hugged Maryellen, who was already hugging Angela. The three of them bounced up and down with excitement, their arms all tangled up together.

Maryellen turned to say thank you to Davy, but Wayne was raising one of Davy's hands in the air, as if he had won a prizefight.

"I had no idea what Ellie and Davy were doing," said Karen Stohlman to Angela. "I never would have gotten France if it weren't for *your* clue. Thank you so much!"

"You mean *grazie*. That's how you say 'thank you' in Italian," Maryellen told Karen.

Karen hesitated, and then she grinned. "*Grazie*, Angela," she said. "And *grazie*, Ellie, too."

✳

For winning the Geography Bee, every member of Team Two got a ball-shaped yo-yo that had a map of the world on it, just like a globe.

Davy won everyone's admiration because he could make his yo-yo do a trick called "Around the World." "I'm doing 'Around the World' at the same time that I'm making the world go around because my yo-yo is a globe," Davy announced as the class lined up to go to the cafeteria.

Maryellen grinned at him, and she thought he sort of grinned back, but it was so quick, she wasn't sure.

Karen Stohlman asked Maryellen and Angela, "Have you two been secretly studying geography?"

"No, but during our Lunch Bunch lessons we used maps for fun so that Angela could learn English and I could practice my handwriting," Maryellen explained.

"Well, you two seem to know the whole world!" said Karen King.

"Except for Chile and Bolivia," Angela said softly, and everyone laughed.

Then Karen Stohlman asked Maryellen and Angela shyly, "Want to sit together at lunch?"

"Okay," said Angela.

"Sure!" said Maryellen. Her heart flooded with forgiveness for the Karens. They hadn't come right out and said that they were sorry, but they were showing that they wanted to be her friend again—and Angela's friend, too.

"Angela, you've certainly learned a lot of English," said Karen King.

"Ellie taught me," said Angela. "She made it fun."

Maryellen grinned at Angela. Then she sighed and said, "I just wish my handwriting had improved as much as Angela's English has. Mrs. Humphrey probably wishes that, too. I mean, that was the whole reason she asked me to come to Lunch Bunch."

✳

When Maryellen and Angela arrived for Lunch Bunch time, neither Davy nor Mrs. Humphrey was there yet. The girls decided to work on sentences.

"If something happened in the past, you use *was*," said Maryellen. "Like, 'The Geography Bee *was* fun.'

But if the thing is happening now, you use *is*. Like, 'Angela *is* smart.' Now you try."

"Okay," said Angela. "How about: 'Davy is your friend.'"

Maryellen smiled sadly, and gently corrected Angela. "Davy *was* my friend," she said.

Angela shook her head firmly. "No," she said. "He *is*."

"Well," Maryellen sighed. "Let's just say that I hope that maybe someday, he *will be* my friend again. *Will be* is what you say when you're talking about the future, and the things you hope for."

When Mrs. Humphrey and Davy arrived, Mrs. Humphrey told Davy and Angela that they could go to recess, and then she called Maryellen to her desk.

"Maryellen," Mrs. Humphrey said, without any Care, Jo, no, or ohs!, as if she knew *exactly* who Maryellen was without any doubt now. "You and Angela have had a good time helping each other, haven't you?"

"Oh, yes!" said Maryellen. "We're good friends."

"Splendid," said Mrs. Humphrey. She hesitated, and then she went on, "It was kind of you to befriend

Angela, and it was brave, too. I saw how your old friends disapproved. It's not easy to take a stand when you have to stand apart."

Maryellen nodded, pleased that her teacher had noticed what was going on. "I think we're all friends now, though."

"Good," said Mrs. Humphrey. She began leafing through the composition book with Maryellen's sketches and labels in it. "I know that you have been trying for quite some time to change your handwriting, and I appreciate your effort. But I think that loopy style you invented for yourself actually looks better than your attempts at normal cursive. Just keep doing what you're doing. You're you, with your own individual way of doing things, so I guess it makes sense that your handwriting is unique, too." She handed the book back to Maryellen.

"Thanks!" said Maryellen, hugging the book to her chest. *That's me*, she thought, *I'm the one-and-only Maryellen Larkin, and there's no one else quite like me in the whole wide world.*

Christmas Is on Its Way, Hurray!

✳ CHAPTER TEN ✳

t was several weeks later when Maryellen climbed up onto the workbench in the carport and sang to Scooter: "On the first day of Christmas my true love gave to me, a partridge in a pear tree."

Even though it was a hot, sunny afternoon, Maryellen could *feel* the shivery excitement of Christmas beginning. It seemed to her that right after Thanksgiving, the whole world's heart had started to beat a little faster, and there was a sparky feeling of happy anticipation in the air. Already the stores were bright with lights and merry with the sound of Christmas music. Magazines were fat with photos of luscious Christmas dinners and living rooms beautifully decorated with candles and holly. Every day the mail brought Christmas cards with glittery illustrations of old-fashioned sleighs dashing through the snow. TV commercials showed happy families shopping, their arms full of wrapped presents, or later, opening the presents under the piney, shiny Christmas tree. Maryellen studied every picture and every detail and took it all to heart. She imagined herself in every TV show, every commercial, and every movie about Christmas, as if it were her own life.

As she moved boxes on the shelves above the workbench, she sang, "On the second day of Christmas, my true love gave to me—"

"Ellie-kelly," Joan interrupted. "Are you singing a Christmas song already?" Joan was strolling up the driveway with an armload of books, on her way back from a study date with *her* true love, Jerry. She leaned against the workbench and smiled at Maryellen. "Isn't it a bit early?"

"No," Maryellen said happily. "It's December at last. Christmas is on its way." There was no question about it: Christmas was Maryellen's absolute favorite time of year. Surprises! Presents! Decorations! Grandmom and Grandpop visiting! Wishes coming true! That's what Christmas was. Maryellen thought about Christmas and planned for it and looked forward to it all year long. She put five cents of her allowance aside every single week in the Christmas Club at the bank for Christmas shopping. She kept a list of gifts for her family and added to it whenever she had a good idea, even in the summer. As soon as the winter edition of the Sears-Roebuck catalog came, she went through it page by page with Beverly, Tom, and Mikey and helped them choose what they wanted. Then she helped them write their letters to Santa.

Maryellen said to Joan, "Mom said we could start to put up our Christmas decorations tonight when Dad gets home from work." She pulled a box labeled "Christmas" off the top shelf. "Can you help me take the boxes inside?"

"Sure," said Joan. She put her books down and peered into the box that Maryellen handed to her. "Oh, look! Here are the paper snowflakes we made for the tree last year." Joan shook the box a little and jingle bells rang, which made Scooter tilt his head and lift his ears. "The jingle bells are in this box, too."

"Jingle bells remind me of wedding bells," said Maryellen. She grinned at Joan. "Christmas is romantic. Wouldn't it be wonderful if Jerry gave you an engagement ring for Christmas?"

"Well, yes," said Joan. Then she laughed. "Anyway, I'd rather get a ring than a partridge in a pear tree!"

Maryellen described the scene the way she had seen it in movies: "You'll be in front of the Christmas tree, just the two of you. There'll be candlelight, and Christmas music playing in the background. You're wearing a beautiful evening gown, like the one Rosemary Clooney wore in *White Christmas*. Jerry will get down on bended knee, and hold up a little box with a diamond ring in it, and say—"

"Whoa!" Joan interrupted. "Hold your horses, Ellie-nelly. You're letting your imagination run away with you. It's Jerry's decision whether he's going to propose or not."

"I know," said Maryellen. "It's just that I love Christmas so much. And if you and Jerry got engaged . . . well, it would make Christmas perfect."

"I love Christmas, too," said Joan with a smile. "So let's take these boxes inside."

"Okay," said Maryellen. She looked inside the biggest box. "This box has our Christmas tree in it."

Instead of a real fir tree, the Larkins put up an artificial tree with wire branches and pink plastic needles. The tree was six feet tall, and was permanently attached to its white wooden base.

As Maryellen looked at the tree, she had the most unexpected reaction. Always before, she had been excited about the tree, and had thought it was very pretty. But now, rather than the happy thrill that she expected, she felt—there was no denying it—a teeny, tiny twinge of disappointment. For one thing, no one on TV or in the movies ever got engaged in front of a pink plastic tree. "Uh, Joan?" she began slowly. It was in Maryellen's mind to ask Joan if she was ever sorry that their family didn't have a tree like the ones in all the movies, TV shows, and magazine photos: a traditional, deep-green pine tree that was *real*. But she stopped herself before she asked the question out loud.

"What?" asked Joan.

"Nothing," said Maryellen quickly. How disloyal of her to be disappointed in her family's tree! How un-Christmassy to be critical!

"Come on, then, Ellie-belle," said Joan. "Time to get Christmas going."

"Right!" said Maryellen. Joan helped her lower the Christmas tree box to the floor, and then Maryellen climbed down from the workbench, stepping over Scooter. She put her fleeting feeling of disappointment behind her as solidly as she put her two feet on the ground. But somehow, as she dragged the tree box inside, the feeling seemed to lurk like a shadow, no matter how hard she tried to forget it.

✳

"Dad," said Beverly, "how will Santa bring our presents if we don't have a chimney?"

It was later, after dinner, and the whole Larkin family was together, decorating the living room. Maryellen remembered worrying about the "no chimney" problem when she was little. Tom and Mikey looked at Dad anxiously.

"Don't worry," said Mr. Larkin. "Santa knows that houses here in Florida don't need fireplaces or chimneys because it's never very cold. So he comes in the back door, and reads the Christmas Wish letters you leave for him next to your stockings on the bookshelf. And his reindeer graze on the lawn and have a snack while Santa puts your presents under the tree."

"In fact," said Mrs. Larkin, "I bet Santa likes Florida best of all, because he can land his sleigh on the ground. When I was a kid back in the mountains in Georgia, I used to worry about him landing his sleigh on our rooftop. It was awfully slippery with all that ice and snow on it."

"Is there always snow at Christmastime up in the mountains?" asked Maryellen.

"Just about always," said Mrs. Larkin. "We usually had a white Christmas when I was a kid."

"Oh," said Maryellen enviously. "How wonderful!"

Mom smiled. "Our Christmases were pretty quiet and simple back then," she said. "It was during the Depression, and no one had any money."

Dad spoke up. "Your mother and I are happy to be able to buy gifts for you kids, to go all-out at Christmas and try our best to make all your wishes come true," he said, "since we had to scrimp when we were growing up."

"But you know your grandmom and grandpop," said Mrs. Larkin. "They could make fun out of an old brown bag if they had to! We'd hike up the mountain and choose a tree, and Grandpop would chop it down. I was always a little sorry that we didn't leave the tree outside, so that the branches could still be covered with snow. To me, the snow was the prettiest decoration of all. So white and glittery! But I did love how the tree made the whole house smell piney inside. And Grandpop always lifted me onto his shoulders to put the star at the very top of the tree. I loved that, too."

"This year it's *my* turn," crowed Beverly happily. She spun on her toes. "Grandpop is going to lift *me* up and *I* will put the star at the top of our tree."

Maryellen wanted to ask Mom more questions about what Christmas was like when she was a little girl, but just then, the phone rang. Mom hurried to the kitchen to answer it. When she returned, she and Dad exchanged a worried look.

"What's the matter?" Maryellen asked.

Mom's voice was sad. "That was Grandpop on the phone," she said. "And—"

Beverly interrupted. "Did you remind him that it's *me* he'll be lifting?"

"Oh, Beverly, honey," said Mom. "I'm afraid . . . I'm afraid he won't."

"How come?" asked Beverly.

"Why not?" asked Maryellen at exactly the same moment.

Mom sighed. "You know that Grandpop was sick this fall."

"But he's fine now," said Maryellen. "I've been sending him homemade get-well cards every week, and when he writes back to thank me for them, he always says he's feeling better."

"I know, dear," said Mom. "But just now on the phone, he said that he wasn't quite up to the train trip here, or all the holiday hoopla. He and Grandmom think it'll be best if they stay home in Georgia and have a quiet Christmas. They won't be coming to visit us."

"Oh no," wailed all the children except Mikey, who looked confused. Maryellen was so crushed that she thought she couldn't *stand* it.

"Poor Grandmom and Grandpop," said Dad sadly. "Their Christmas will be awfully quiet. They'll be all by themselves. It'll hardly feel like Christmas at all."

"*Our* Christmas will hardly feel like Christmas, either, without Grandmom and Grandpop here," said Maryellen, her voice choked with sorrow.

"Yes," said Carolyn. "Who will make Grandmom's Christmas coffee cake? And who will sing Christmas songs all day long, like Grandpop always does?"

"Who will lift me up to put the star on the top of the tree if Grandpop isn't here?" moped Beverly.

"Hey!" said Dad. "What's all this grousing? You girls can help your mother make the coffee cake, and listen to this." Dad picked up the jingle bells and shook them as he sang at the top of his voice: "Jingle bells, jingle bells, jingle all the way!"

Pretty soon, Dad had everyone singing along. When the song ended, Dad said, "And don't worry, Queen Beverly. I'll lift you up. You won't miss out on your *starring* role."

Maryellen laughed at Dad's pun, along with everyone else. But she couldn't shake off her deep disappointment about Grandmom and Grandpop, just as she couldn't shake off her disappointment about the fake, wire-and-plastic tree. Now that it was upright, and its branches were outspread, and it was decorated with ornaments, the tree seemed even pinker and faker than she'd remembered. It had no piney scent, no feathery green needles, no solid wooden trunk. It was so very different from the fragrant, live tree Mom had described!

A sigh escaped Maryellen. "You really had the right kind of Christmas when you were a kid, Mom."

"What do you mean by 'the right kind'?" asked Dad. "What's wrong with our Christmas? Don't you like it?"

"Oh, sure I do!" said Maryellen quickly. With eight people in her house, there were always lots of presents piled under the tree. There were even presents for Scooter! Maryellen and all of her sisters and brothers banded together and made presents for their parents. One year it was kites. Last year it was gingerbread men that looked like themselves and a gingerbread dog to be Scooter. This year, it was going to be a poster of their handprints and Scooter's paw prints forming a big heart.

Their family *did* fun stuff, too. On Christmas Eve afternoon, Dad and all the kids dashed off to O'Neal's department store for last-minute shopping and then had ice cream afterward. When it was dark, the whole family went to the beach. Joan's boyfriend Jerry came, too, and helped Dad build a bonfire. They sang carols, and Dad read "'Twas the Night Before Christmas" aloud. On Christmas morning, they went to a sunrise church service on the pier. Then, for breakfast, they had Grandmom's coffee cake accompanied by juicy Florida oranges. Maryellen's family had lots of great traditions, and Maryellen remembered every single one and treasured them all. And yet . . . "It's just that in songs and stories and TV shows, Christmas is always cold and snowy," she explained.

"Ah," said Dad. "You mean, Christmas should look old-fashioned and traditional."

"Yes," said Maryellen. "I guess I do."

"Well, Ellie," said Mom, "America is a big country. The cold, snowy Christmas isn't possible for lots of people, not only us."

"But I know what Ellie is getting at," said Joan. Now that Joan was eighteen and practically engaged, everyone listened to her as if she were a grown-up. "Here in Florida, we put our own twist on Christmas. We spray pretend snow out of a can onto the windows. We put red bows on palm trees. Our presents are snorkels and beach balls, not sleds and skis. We sing about snow, we recite poems about snow, we tell stories about snow, but

we don't have a flake of snow all winter. I think what
Ellie is saying is that our Christmas isn't quite right. It
isn't like Christmas in any of the books that we read.
Our Christmas isn't . . . well, *Christmassy*."

"There's no *right* way to celebrate Christmas," said
Dad. "We celebrate our way, and our way is nice."

*Nice, but **different**,* thought Maryellen stubbornly.

One thing Maryellen did not like about growing
up was that she saw everything with new eyes. She
felt awkward, as if she was standing outside her family looking in. But she couldn't help it. She knew what
Christmas was supposed to look like, and this year, for
the first time, she realized that her family's Christmas
did not look right.

"Just once," she said wistfully, "I wish that I could
have a *real* Christmas, a perfect Christmas, a Christmas
that's snowy, the way it's *supposed* to be."

✳

The next afternoon after school, Maryellen was
sitting on the floor in the living room with Beverly
on one side, Tom on the other, and Mikey in her lap.
Scooter, who was always glad to do anything that did

not include moving, snoozed at her feet. Maryellen
had promised to help the little kids by writing their
Christmas Wish letters to Santa for them, and they
were looking at the Sears-Roebuck catalog to get ideas.
When they saw something that they liked, Maryellen
marked it with a star and turned down the corner of
the page. So far, she had starred a toy fireman's hat
for Tom, and for Beverly, a fairy queen costume with
wings and a sparkly wand.

"What do *you* want, Mikey?" Maryellen asked.

"Tick-tock!" said Mikey. That was his word for Mr.
Larkin's wristwatch, which fascinated him for some
reason.

"No," said Beverly, brisk and superior. "You're too
little for a wristwatch. You can't tell time, like Ellie and
I can."

Mikey's face fell. Even though Beverly was quite
right, Maryellen felt sorry for Mikey. Quickly, she got
scissors and tape. She flipped to the page of men's
watches. It was easy to find; she'd already turned
down its corner because next to the watches there were
engagement rings that she thought Joan might like to
see. Maryellen cut a man's watch out of the catalog, and

taped it around Mikey's wrist. "There!" she said.

"Tick-tock," said Mikey, perfectly pleased with his paper watch. He held it up to show Beverly, saying, "Tick-tock, tick-tock, tick-tock!"

"Okay, okay!" said Beverly. She rolled her eyes to make it clear that *she* was far too smart and grown-up to fall for a paper watch cut out of a catalog, for heaven's sake.

"Now, Mikey," said Maryellen kindly, "you'll have to think of something *else* you'd like."

"Cookie!" said Mikey. Scooter lifted his head at the sound of one of his favorite words, and Tom and Maryellen laughed. Mikey thought he'd said something clever and funny, so he said it again. "Cookie!"

Beverly sighed with exasperation. "You can't ask Santa for a cookie!" She opened the catalog to a page that had stuffed animals on it and said, "You have to ask for a toy, like a stuffed animal or something. You know, like your teddy bear."

"Bear!" said Mikey joyfully. "Teddy bear."

"You already *have* a teddy bear," Maryellen pointed out gently.

"Bear!" said Mikey, looking fierce. "BEAR!"

✳ The One and Only ✳

"Ohhh-kay," said Maryellen. For a guy with a lim-
ited vocabulary, Mikey sure was good at making his
desires clear! She put a star next to the teddy bear that
looked exactly like the one Mikey already had, except a
lot cleaner, and folded the corner of the page.

"Have you chosen what *you'd* like, Ellie?" asked
Mom. She and Carolyn were hanging Christmas cards
on a string over the doorway.

"Oh, yes," said Maryellen. "I've known for a long
time."

"May I see?" asked Mom.

"Sure," said Maryellen. She turned to the page that
she had folded back and pointed to a starred picture of
a white leather jewelry box. The box was open so that
you could see that it was lined in white velvet dusted
with silver snowflakes. A little skater, wearing a short
red skating skirt, scarf, and stocking cap, stood on one
toe on a pond made of a round mirror. "When you lift
the lid, music plays and the little skater twirls around
as if she's skating on the little mirror," Maryellen
explained. "I love her because she's so pretty and
Christmassy."

"I saw a jewelry box like that in O'Neal's," said

Carolyn. "The music is 'The Skaters' Waltz,' and the little skater looks sort of like a ballerina."

"I'm a ballerina!" exclaimed Beverly. "Everybody look at me!" Beverly leapt to her feet and twirled on tiptoe with her arms raised above her head.

Everyone clapped, but without much enthusiasm. Beverly took ballet lessons, and they were all pretty tired of being commanded to watch her dance.

Maryellen wasn't really paying any attention to Beverly at all. Instead, she was staring hard at the photo of the jewelry-box skater. She could almost feel herself gliding gracefully on a frozen pond surrounded by glistening, sparkling snow, under a wintry sky, in sharp, cold wintry air.

Maryellen felt Mom's hand on her shoulder. "That little skater *is* very pretty and Christmassy," Mom said dreamily, as she looked at the photograph, too. "I used to ice-skate on a frozen pond like that with Grandmom and Grandpop when I was your age." The faraway, sad tone in Mom's voice reminded Maryellen that Mom was as heartbroken as she was that Grandmom and Grandpop weren't coming for Christmas. Then Mom tousled Maryellen's hair and joked, "It's too bad we don't have any ice-skating rinks here in Daytona Beach. Now, if that little jewelry-box skater were waterskiing, we'd be all set. *That* we can do on a Florida Christmas!"

Four Wishes
Rolled into One

✷ CHAPTER ELEVEN ✷

After Maryellen finished writing her letter to Santa, she wandered out to the carport, still daydreaming about the jewelry-box skater. The vision of the little skater enchanted her, and the snowy pond seemed almost more real to her than the carport. She strapped on her roller skates. Gliding forward, she pretended that her roller skates were ice skates and that she was gliding on a glassy frozen pond hidden in the mountains instead of a hot, concrete driveway in flat Florida. Humming a waltz under her breath, Maryellen leaned forward on her right foot and lifted her left leg behind her, in the same pose as the little skater in the jewelry box. She closed her eyes, and . . . *kerplunk*! She fell hard, scraping one knee and the palms of both hands on the concrete.

Carolyn burst out of the kitchen door and rushed

toward Maryellen. Beverly, who couldn't bear to miss anything Maryellen was up to, was close behind. "Gosh, Ellie, are you okay?" Carolyn asked.

"Sure," said Maryellen, dusting herself off, feeling a little foolish in front of Carolyn and Beverly. "I was just, uh, just—"

"You were pretending to be that jewelry-box ice-skater ballerina," Beverly announced in her piping voice, "skating on a snowy pond at Christmastime."

Hmph! thought Maryellen. How annoying— Beverly was so nosy that she even poked her nose into Maryellen's private daydreams! "I know it's silly," she admitted.

Carolyn shrugged. "Hey, I used to pretend that my bike was a horse," she said. "I'd put little piles of grass in front of it for it to eat." Maryellen chuckled, and Carolyn went on. "I can help you," she said. "I'll play 'The Skaters' Waltz' on the piano really loud so that you can skate to it out here in the carport. It'll be fun!"

"Okay," said Maryellen. "Thanks!"

"I can help you, too!" said Beverly, tugging on Maryellen's sleeve so that she'd look at her. "I know ballet. I can teach you."

Maryellen hesitated. She was not sure that she wanted instructions from Queen Beverly the Bossy. But Beverly *did* take ballet, and she was already strapping on a pair of roller skates. There was no stopping her. Reluctantly, Maryellen said, "Well, I guess so."

Carolyn bounded inside, leaving the side door open, and began pounding away at the piano. She was a very enthusiastic piano player, but not a very good one. Her playing was sort of stop-and-start, herky-jerky, and off-key, but it was definitely *loud*.

As Beverly skated next to Maryellen, she shouted over the din, "Chin up! Back straight! Tummy in! Put one arm out in front and the other in back. No! Not stiff like that, like *this*." Beverly extended her arms gracefully, curving them just a little at the elbows and lifting her hands at the wrists. Maryellen could tell that Beverly was imitating her ballet teacher, Madame La Fleur, when she said, "Now lift your back leg in an *arabesque*. Not so high! Glide, *glissade*! Chin *up*."

Maryellen tried hard to move like Beverly (who, it annoyed her to admit, looked good), but she felt awkward and oafish. Even Scooter, who waddled like an overweight duck when he walked, looked at her clumsy skating in dismay.

But once, for a few moments, Maryellen managed to skate smoothly and to lift one foot behind her slowly and smoothly, too. She made up her own words to the tune of "The Skaters' Waltz" in her head: *Flying along, sliding on ice . . .* At that moment, she thought, *This is what it would feel like!* She imagined herself skating on a small pond, surrounded by snowy woods, just as the sun was setting so that the snow was tinted pink, just like on a Christmas card . . .

"*Encore*, Ellie!" Beverly's needle-sharp voice pierced Maryellen's daydream and dragged her back to reality. "That means do it again."

✳

When Maryellen slid into her seat at the dinner table that night, she saw a pretty Christmas card next to her plate. It had a picture of a snowy house on it. Glitter sprinkled on top of the painted snow caught the light and sparkled like real snowflakes.

"What's Ellie got?" Beverly asked immediately.

"Oh," said Mom, looking over her shoulder as she dished up spaghetti. "Grandmom sent me the recipe for the coffee cake, and she tucked that card for Ellie in the envelope. It's from Grandpop."

"Why didn't I get one?" asked Beverly.

"You didn't write to Grandpop," said Joan. "Ellie did."

"What does it say?" asked Carolyn.

Maryellen opened the card and read aloud:

> *Dear Ellie,*
>
> *Merry-almost-Christmas! We are sorry we won't see you this year.*
>
> *Thank you for your get-well card. Your drawing of Scooter sleeping is so good that I can almost hear him snoring!*
>
> *It snowed here last night. Now our house looks just like the one on this Christmas card!*
>
> *Love, Grandpop*
> *XOXOXO, Grandmom, too!*

Dad glanced over at the picture on Grandpop's card and whistled. "Wow, that's a lot of snow!" he said.

Maryellen stared at the illustration of the snowy

house. Smoke curled up from its chimney, yellow light spilled out its windows and cast a glow on the snowy ground outside, and evergreen trees heavily laden with snow leaned toward the house as if they were protecting it. It was so perfect! She longed to walk into the snowy scene. Suddenly, she had an inspiration so brilliant it made her heart beat faster. *Maybe*, she thought, *I can make all **four** of my Christmas wishes come true!*

Trying to sound calm, she said, "It must be awfully cold up there in the mountains, right?"

"You bet!" said Dad. "Brr!" He pretended to shiver. He disliked the cold.

"Is it cold enough that the ponds are frozen?" Maryellen asked.

"I guess so," said Dad, a bit distracted now because he was helping Tom twirl a forkful of spaghetti against his spoon.

"Would the ponds be frozen hard enough to skate on?" Maryellen asked.

Mom looked up from wiping spaghetti sauce off Mikey, who liked to eat his noodles with his hands. "Why are you asking all these questions, Ellie my dear?" she asked.

"I know! I know!" cried Beverly. She raised her hand as if she were in school, except that her hand held a fork with two meatballs on it. Scooter, lurking nearby, followed her fork with his eyes, confident that sooner or later a meatball would fall.

"I'm asking Ellie, not you, Beverly," said Mom.

Everyone turned toward Maryellen, who took a deep breath. Her idea was so *new* that she wasn't quite ready to say it out loud yet, but it was so *good* that it made her feel lit up like a Christmas tree inside. Impulsively, she plunged in, saying, "I was just thinking. What if I wrote to Grandmom and Grandpop and asked if I could come to their house for Christmas? I could take the train, and—"

Now everyone started talking at once.

"What?"

"Go where?"

"I want to go, too!"

"For Christmas?"

"By yourself?"

"On the train?"

"Choo-choo train!" yelled Mikey. "Choo-oo, choo! Choo-oo choo!"

Scooter howled, *"Ar-roo! Ar-roo-oo!"*

"Settle down, kids," said Dad, holding up his hands. "You, too, Scooter." When it was quiet, Dad turned to Maryellen, looking puzzled. "Your heart is so set on a snowy Christmas that you'd go away?" he asked.

"Well, it's not only the snow," Maryellen said, "though that *is* my Wish Number One. I also wish I could be with Grandmom and Grandpop. And I'd love, just once, to have a traditional Christmas like Mom used to have, with a real tree. My fourth wish is that maybe their pond will be frozen, so—"

"So you can skate like the jewelry-box ballerina!" Beverly blurted out. "It will be so pretty! I want to go, too! I want a snowy Christmas and skating on a pond! Please, can't I go, too?"

"Let's not get carried away," said Mom. "No one's going anywhere *yet*."

"Right!" said Dad. "I'm not so keen about this plan. We'd miss you around here, Ellie honey! You're our jolliest Christmas elf. And stop to think: If you go to Grandmom and Grandpop's, you'll miss our traditional last-minute shopping trip to O'Neal's, with ice cream afterward."

"You'll miss the bonfire on the beach with Jerry," said Joan. "And singing carols."

"You won't be here when I read 'Twas the Night Before Christmas,'" said Dad. He recited from the poem: "'*The moon on the breast of the new-fallen snow gave the luster of mid-day to objects below.*' And you won't be here on Christmas Day morning to open presents under the tree with us."

Maryellen began, "Dad, I—"

Dad held up his hand to stop her. "Your mother and I will discuss your idea after dinner," he said firmly. "Now, who's ready for dessert?" Dad inspected everyone's plate. Most everyone still had loops of spaghetti and puddles of sauce. "Hmph!" said Dad. "You've all been too busy gabbing to eat. So far, only Scooter is a member of the Clean Plate Club. Eat up, kids! I hear there's butterscotch pudding for dessert."

✶

Later, when Mom came in to tuck Maryellen into bed, she said, "Your father and I talked about your idea. We've decided that you may write to Grandmom and Grandpop—"

"Oh! Mom, thanks!" Maryellen interrupted.

Mom went on, "If they say yes—which is a big if, what with Grandpop being ill—you may go from Christmas Eve until New Year's Eve. You'll have to pay half of your train fare yourself, but Dad and I will pay the other half. That will be your main Christmas present. Okay?"

"Yes!" said Maryellen joyfully. She flung her arms around Mom. "Thank you, thank you, thank you, Mom."

"Dad's right, we'll miss you," Mom said. "But I convinced him that you would cheer up Grandmom and Grandpop, and I'd feel better about them, knowing they're not alone for Christmas."

Beverly sat up straight in her bed and protested, "Ellie always gets to do the best things! It's not fair. Why can't I go, too, Mom?"

"Beverly, honeybun," said Mom gently. "This is Ellie's wish. It's her idea, and so it will be her adventure, if it happens at all. Anyway, Dad and I couldn't possibly spare *two* of you. It'll be hard enough to do without Ellie. How could our Christmas be merry without our Beverly?"

"Hmph!" grumped Beverly, not sounding very merry at all. She flopped back down onto her pillow.

"Cheer up, Beverly," said Joan, looking over the top of her book. "I'm sure there'll be some nice Christmas surprises for you, right here at home."

After Mom left, Maryellen was too excited to sleep. She slipped out of bed and took writing paper and a pen to the living room. She checked the train schedule that Mom kept in her desk. Then she wrote:

> *Dear Grandmom and Grandpop,*
>
> *Hello! How are you? We hope that you are feeling better, Grandpop. Thank you for the pretty card that you sent.*
>
> *Now I have a big favor to ask: Please may I come see you for Christmas? I just can't imagine a Christmas without you two in it! And the other things I want most in the whole world are a white Christmas with snow, a real pine Christmas tree, and to ice-skate on a frozen pond as the sun is setting on Christmas Eve. I am practicing skating already.*

The train leaves from Daytona Beach on Thursday, December 23rd, at 7:05 p.m. and arrives in Atlanta on Friday, December 24th, at 6:30 a.m. Friday is Christmas Eve!

Oh, please say yes, I can come and stay until New Year's Eve! If I do, I will never forget this Christmas my whole life long.

Love from your granddaughter,
Ellie

P.S. Here is a sketch of Scooter dreaming about meatballs instead of sugarplums.

Maryellen was putting the finishing touches on her sketch when Dad came into the living room. "Writing to your grandparents already, sport?" he asked. Maryellen nodded. "May I read your letter?"

"Sure," said Maryellen. She addressed the envelope, licked the stamp, and put it on the envelope while Dad read the letter.

"This is a good letter," said Dad. He folded it and handed it back to Maryellen. "I guess I can kind of

understand why you want to go on this trip. I have an
itchy foot, too. I like to travel. I've never taken the train
up to the mountains. So if you do go, promise you'll tell
me all about it afterward."

"I promise," said Maryellen.

"And you're really sure that a snowy, TV-show kind
of Christmas is what you truly want?" Dad asked.

"Oh yes, I'm really truly sure!" said Maryellen, with
all her heart.

"Okeydokey," said Dad. He kissed Maryellen on the
forehead. "Then I'll mail your letter for you tomorrow,
and keep my fingers crossed for you, too. Since this is
your four wishes rolled into one, I hope it'll come true."

"Thanks, Dad," said Maryellen. She slid the folded
letter into the envelope, licked the flap, and sealed it
shut.

✳

Only a few days after Maryellen had mailed her letter to Grandmom and Grandpop, the phone rang.

"Ellie, it's for you," Mom called out. She smiled as
she handed the phone to Maryellen.

"Hello?" said Maryellen.

"Is this Ellie, my best girl?" Grandpop asked in his gravelly drawl. "Listen, darlin', you'd be the best present your grandmom and I could hope for. We'd love it if you'd come from Christmas Eve until New Year's Eve."

"Oh, thank you, Grandpop!" said Maryellen. "Are you sure you feel well enough?"

"I think I can manage a visit from a sweetie pie like you," said Grandpop. "In fact, it'll be jim-dandy to have a youngster in the house again. Your grandmom's got a new bird feeder she's wild to show you, and I'll dust off the checkerboard so's you and I can play."

"Oh, thank you!" said Maryellen again. "And Grandpop, is there plenty of snow?"

"Yes-sir-ee-bob!" said Grandpop. "No problem there! And there's a frozen pond for you to skate on, too. I can fix you up with my old hockey skates, or you can just slip 'n' slide in your rain boots. You'll do fine. Now hand the phone over to your mother, Ellie darlin', and we'll firm up this plan."

"Okay! Bye," said Maryellen. "And Grandpop, thanks again." She gave the phone back to Mom and spun a little spin of happiness. Soon she wasn't going to have to *imagine* herself in a scene as perfect as one on TV or a Christmas card; soon she'd really be in it. *It is going to happen,* she thought. *My wish for a perfect Christmas is going to come true!*

✳

The next morning before school began, Maryellen told the Karens and Angela about her trip. Word shot around the playground, and Maryellen became sort of a celebrity. Kids she hardly knew gathered around her and stared. She was pleased to see Davy hovering at the edge of the group. She couldn't even remember what their fight was about anymore, and she was always hoping that she and Davy could be friends again.

"You're going all the way to Atlanta on the train?" said Angela. "All by yourself? And overnight?"

"Yup," said Maryellen. Davy and Wayne, who had replaced Maryellen as Davy's best friend, looked up from the comic book they were sharing, so she could tell that they were listening to the conversation about her trip, even if they were pretending not to.

"Will you have a little roomette of your own?" asked Karen Stohlman.

Maryellen nodded.

"What's a roomette?" asked Karen King.

"It's a wonderful private compartment on the train," explained Karen Stohlman. "It has two seats in it, and the porter turns the seats into a bed for you at night."

"Oooh," murmured the kids in the crowd.

"It will be just like in the movies," sighed Angela.

"When you are sitting, be sure to face forward, Ellie," advised Karen King. "Once we took the train to go see my aunt in St. Augustine and I had to sit facing backward, and I was sick the whole way. And don't get off at the wrong station or anything."

Wayne snorted at Karen's fussy advice. But Maryellen just said, "I won't."

"Are you going to eat in the dining car," Karen King fretted on, "with people you don't even know?" She shuddered. "I wouldn't be able to eat a thing!"

"Mee-yow!" meowed Wayne. He singsonged, "Karen is a scaredy-cat."

"I *am* too much of a scaredy-cat to travel by myself," said Karen. "Ellie's brave."

The kids in the crowd murmured in agreement. Maryellen caught Davy's eye, and he nodded, just the slightest bit.

"And when you get to your grandparents' house, you're going to skate on a pond," gushed Karen Stohlman. "Do you know how to ice-skate?"

"Beverly's teaching me on our roller skates," said Maryellen. "She says it's like ballet."

"Oh, show me!" said Karen Stohlman, who also took ballet lessons with Madame La Fleur as Beverly did.

Everyone watched as Maryellen demonstrated her arabesques and glissades as well as she could in her school shoes on the grass of the playground.

"Hah!" scoffed Wayne. "You look like a baller*rhino*, not a baller*rina*."

"Don't listen to him," said Angela. "I think you look really good."

Karen Stohlman did an arabesque like Maryellen's. "I wish *I* could skate on a frozen pond in the snow," she said. "It sounds so pretty."

"Just don't fall through the ice the way Amy does in *Little Women*," warned Karen King, who took a dim view of dangerous escapades. "And don't get lost in an avalanche or a horrible snowstorm."

"Snow is not horrible; it is beautiful," said Angela, who was the expert on snow because she was the only one who had seen it before. "I wish you could bring back a snowman and some snowballs, Ellie."

"Me, too!" laughed Maryellen. She was pleased to have her friends envy her, and rather tickled to have a reputation as a daring traveler. Even Davy was clearly impressed. Oh, she couldn't *wait* for her adventure to begin!

All Aboard

The next few weeks were very busy for Maryellen. It was as if she was getting ready for *two* Christmases, because she had to get her Christmas presents ready for everyone at home *and* she had to get ready for her trip to Grandmom and Grandpop's. Plus, Beverly insisted on practicing skating as often as possible. She had taken to wearing an old stocking cap she'd found packed away in Mom's closet. The hat reeked of mothballs, but it had a pom-pom on the end of it, just as the little jewelry-box skater's hat did.

"Put your skates on, Ellie," Beverly said one afternoon. "Time for our practice."

"I'll be there in a minute," said Maryellen. She and Carolyn and Scooter were in the girls' bedroom, and Carolyn was helping Maryellen with some Christmas math. They ignored Beverly, who sighed and stomped away, her pom-pom bouncing.

"The train fare from Daytona Beach to Atlanta is thirty-two dollars round-trip," said Carolyn. "But you're under twelve, so you only have to pay half fare, which is sixteen dollars. And Mom and Dad are going to pay half of that, so you only need eight dollars for your train fare."

Maryellen poured all the money out of her change purse onto Carolyn's bed and counted it. Her heart sank. "There's only six dollars here," she said.

"How much money do you have in your Christmas Club account?" asked Carolyn.

"Two dollars and sixty cents," said Maryellen.

"Okay, so you're all set," said Carolyn, the math whiz. "Use two dollars of it, and you'll have sixty cents for Christmas shopping."

"Oh, I couldn't use Christmas Club money on a train ticket for myself!" said Maryellen. "That'd be selfish. Besides, one of my most favorite things to do is to go Christmas shopping and buy great presents for everybody. How can I do that with only sixty cents?"

✳ All Aboard ✳

"Well, you're good at sketching and arty stuff like that," said Carolyn. "You're the one who came up with our idea for Mom and Dad's present this year, our handprint poster, which came out really well."

That was true. Maryellen looked at the poster, which was drying under Joan's bed. All the kids had dipped their hands in finger paint and pressed them onto a piece of poster paper to form a huge heart. Even Scooter's paw print looked good.

"I bet you can make arty presents for the rest of us," Carolyn went on. "Just think really hard about us, and what we like, and your presents will be just exactly right, and much more personal than store-bought ones."

"I guess so," said Maryellen doubtfully. What choice did she have?

Beverly rolled into the bedroom on her roller skates. "I've been waiting a hundred years," she said. "Come *on*."

"Okay, okay," said Maryellen. She scooped up her money and put it back into her change purse. "I'm coming."

"Hurry *up*," commanded Beverly. "You, too, Carolyn. You have to play for us."

"Yes, ma'am, Queen Beverly, your majesty!" said

Carolyn, with an exaggerated curtsy.

As Beverly rolled off down the hall, Maryellen turned to Carolyn and joked, "We'd better be quick, or it'll be off with our heads!"

✳

The very next day, after skating practice with Beverly, Mom gave Maryellen eight dollars. "Here you go, Ellie," said Mom. "Merry Early Christmas."

"Thanks, Mom," said Maryellen. She folded the eight dollars and carefully put them in her change purse.

"Jerry and I are going downtown to the Seaside Diner," said Joan, tying a headscarf under her chin. "Want a ride?"

"In the hot rod?" asked Maryellen. "Yes, please! Oh boy!"

She trotted outside behind Joan to where Jerry's hot rod was parked, gleaming in the sunshine. Jerry leaned against it, his arms crossed over his chest. *He sure is handsome,* Maryellen thought.

"Your chariot awaits," said Jerry, bowing when he saw Maryellen and Joan. "Where to, ladies?"

"The bank first, please," said Joan, "and then the train station, the diner, and the Five and Ten Cent Store."

"Your wish is my command," said Jerry. He opened the door of the hot rod and took Joan's hand to help her in, holding it longer than was strictly necessary, Maryellen noticed.

Joan giggled, delighted. She sat in the front seat next to Jerry, closer than was strictly necessary, Maryellen noticed again. As they rode to the bank, she was mentally kicking herself for not sitting between Jerry and Joan so that they couldn't be lovey-dovey. Most of the time, she was intrigued by—and sort of in awe of—Joan and Jerry's romantic life. It was so grown-up and thrilling! And of course she still wanted them to get married eventually, so that she could be a bridesmaid. But now that she was going to be away at Christmastime, she definitely did *not* want Joan and Jerry to get engaged in front of the Christmas tree. She'd miss the whole thing!

At the bank, Maryellen withdrew her Christmas Club money and added it to the money from Mom in her change purse. Then Jerry drove to the train station and parked out front so that she could purchase her train ticket. Maryellen was sorry to part with her money and Mom's, but she had to admit that holding the actual train ticket in her hand made her feel very excited and very independent.

The diner was right next to the train station, so they left the car in the station parking lot and went inside. Normally, Maryellen liked to sit at the shiny counter on a high, spinning stool, play songs on the jukebox, and watch the cook slide orders through the pickup window from the kitchen. But today she had to be on the alert. She slid swiftly into the booth and onto the seat next to Joan so that Jerry couldn't sit there. But her ploy to keep the lovebirds apart didn't work out too well. Joan and Jerry sat facing each other across the table and shared a milkshake by putting two straws in it. Maryellen noted nervously that every time Joan leaned forward to take a sip, Jerry leaned forward, too, and their noses touched.

"Joan," Maryellen said briskly. "Will you come with me to the Five and Ten Cent Store?"

"Sure," said Joan.

"What are you buying in there?" asked Jerry.

"Art supplies," said Maryellen.

"Art supplies?" repeated Jerry with pretend horror. "Not red paint, I hope. I'm still the only guy in Daytona Beach with red polka dots on my white tennis shorts. The day you painted the front door red was a disaster."

Joan reached across the table and gave Jerry's shoulder a playful shove. "Don't tease my little sister!" Joan smiled through her eyelashes at Jerry. "Besides, that was the day you finally asked me to wear your fraternity pin. Was *that* a disaster?"

Jerry melted. "No, oh, no," he said. "That was—"

"Come on, Joan," said Maryellen, grabbing Joan's arm and pulling her out of the booth before Jerry could dive across the table and smooch her. "Can we go now?"

"Okay, Ellie-welly," said Joan.

"Hurry back," said Jerry. "I'll meet you at the car."

Maryellen rolled her eyes. Really! It was a challenge to prevent Joan and Jerry from being *mushy*. After Joan helped her buy art supplies and they got in the car with Jerry to ride home, Joan started to sing, "On the first day of Christmas . . ."

Uh-oh! thought Maryellen. The last thing she wanted Joan and Jerry thinking about was true loves and golden rings! So she drowned Joan out, singing the

least romantic song she knew as loud as she could to
distract her:

> *There was a man named Michael Finnegan,*
> *He grew whiskers on his chinnegan.*

Joan and Jerry laughed, and then sang along with her:

> *Shaved them off and they grew in again,*
> *Poor old Michael Finnegan!*

✳

Maryellen thought hard about her sisters and brothers and made a list of presents that she could make
for them. Then came *making* the presents, which was
the fun part, but also the hard part. She didn't want to
give Joan anything wedding-y or bride-y, so she made
her bookmarks that looked like the spines of books
to remind Joan that she loved to read as much as she
loved Jerry.

She painted two clothespins with designs of musi-
cal notes for Carolyn. When Carolyn played the piano,
her sheet music was always blowing closed or slipping

off the music holder. The clothespins would solve that problem!

For Queen Beverly, Maryellen cut a crown out of cardboard. She covered the cardboard in tinfoil, and glued onto it sparkly buttons that looked like jewels.

She made Tom's present out of cardboard, too. She cut out the shape of a fire truck and colored it bright red. Then she made a ladder that really folded up and down, using a two-pronged paper fastener as a hinge.

Mikey was still at the age where he was more excited about the box that a present came in than the present itself, so it was hard to think of a present for him. But Maryellen knew that Mikey liked stuffed animals, so she stuffed soft rags inside one of her old Brownie socks to make Mikey a fat, brown worm.

Scooter was easy. Maryellen wrapped up a dog biscuit for him.

Maryellen imagined how happy her sisters and brothers and Scooter would look when they were opening their presents from her on Christmas morning. She wished that she could see their faces, and she felt a tiny twinge of regret when she remembered that, of course, she wouldn't be there. But she quickly shook it off. *I'll be in the snowy mountains with Grandmom and Grandpop,* she told herself, *having a **real** Christmas.*

✳

The day finally came when all of Maryellen's presents for her family were finished and wrapped and tagged and bowed. She was happily adding them to the pile under the tree when Beverly marched into the room with Carolyn in tow.

"Come on, Ellie," said Beverly. "Time for our skating practice. Carolyn's ready to play for us."

"Okay," said Maryellen, only somewhat enthusiastically. As she followed Beverly to the carport and strapped on her roller skates, she felt a little irritated. Beverly was taking her job as skating instructor too seriously, as if it were a queenly duty and a royal responsibility.

"Stand up straight!" Beverly ordered as Carolyn played "The Skaters' Waltz" and Maryellen tried to glide on one foot the way Beverly did. "Tummy in! Shoulders down! Chin up, no, not too up! Now, *plié.* Cup the fingers gracefully! Curve the arms! Rise up and *arabesque*! Now, *glissade.* Glide."

Maryellen had soon learned that *plié* meant to sort of squat. *Arabesque* meant to skate on one leg with the other sticking straight out behind her, with one arm forward and one arm back. *Glissade* meant glide. And the one Maryellen grew to dread the most, *Encore!* meant do all the moves all over again from the beginning. After a while, her legs ached and her arms felt as heavy and stiff as telephone poles. She had bumps and scrapes and scabs on her hands and knees from all her falls. But Beverly was tough and tireless.

"Encore!" commanded Beverly when Maryellen had fallen for the third time.

Maryellen was fed up. Clearly, the idea of being the big ballet boss was stuck *in* Beverly's head like the pom-pom hat was stuck *on* it. "I'm tired," she said. "Let's stop."

"No," ordered Beverly. "You need more practice. You keep forgetting to lift your chin."

"Quit bossing me around!" said Maryellen.

"Not until you do it right," said Beverly. "Madame La Fleur says—"

"You're not Madame La Fleur," said Maryellen, annoyed. "Right now, you're Madame La Pain."

Beverly's face flushed red. "Don't you understand—"

"Oh, I understand, all right," Maryellen interrupted, rubbing a black-and-blue bruise on her knee. "This is your big chance to show off. You know ballet and I don't."

For a second, Beverly looked as though she might cry. Then her face hardened and she said, "Well, for your information, Miss Smarty-pants, you keep doing it all wrong. You stink! I was only trying to help you be less clumsy."

Now Maryellen's face flushed red. Her feelings were as hurt as her knees. "I don't need your help!" she snapped.

"Hmph! That's what you think," said Beverly. She shrugged. "Go ahead and look terrible. See if I care. I quit."

"Fine by me!" said Maryellen. "I never asked for your help in the first place. You're the one who barged in, as usual. You and your fussy, fancy, French-y words that have taken all the fun out of skating."

"Well, *you're* the one who's ruining everyone's Christmas because of your big dumb idea!" shouted Beverly.

"Hey, hey, hey," said Carolyn as she and Joan and Scooter came outside, swinging the screen door wide. Maryellen and Beverly had been arguing so loudly, they hadn't heard the music stop. "Knock it off, girls."

"I think you're both tired," said Joan. "That's the end of practice for today."

"That's the end of practice for for*ever*!" said Beverly. She skated off down the driveway in a huff, her pom-pom quivering with anger.

"Ack!" exclaimed Maryellen to Joan and Carolyn. "Beverly drives me crazy!"

"Oh, don't mind Queen Beverly," Carolyn said to Maryellen. "I'll go talk to her."

After Carolyn left, Joan said, "Beverly will get over her snit. She loves helping you, and you really are doing better." Then Joan crossed her arms over her chest and surveyed Maryellen. "But you need to dress for the part, Ellie-loo," she said. "Shorts and a T-shirt are all wrong for an ice-skater. You really should have a hat like Beverly's. And . . . " Joan tied her own silk scarf around Maryellen's neck so that the ends fluttered and made it seem as if there were a breeze. "There!" she said. "That's more like it."

"Thanks," said Maryellen. She hesitated, and then she asked, "Do you think I'm being ridiculous? I mean, about having a snowy Christmas and skating and all. Is it a big dumb idea, as Beverly said?"

"It's no goofier than most of your ideas," said Joan, grinning. "In fact, I think Queen Beverly is envious. She wishes she could go with you, and that's why she's being such a pain." Joan paused and then said with a shrug, "But we can't always get what we wish for."

Maryellen wondered if Joan was thinking about her *own* wish for an engagement ring from Jerry. Unlike Mikey's tick-tock, that was a wish that couldn't be fulfilled with a paper ring cut out of the Sears-Roebuck catalog.

✳

Carolyn began, "'Twas the night before . . . "

"Ellie's train trip," finished Tom.

"And all through the house, *lots* of creatures were stirring, trying to help her pack!" joked Carolyn.

It was true. Maryellen was packing, and just about her whole family was in on the act. Carolyn and Tom had balcony seats on the top bunk to watch her put things in her suitcase. Beverly, still standoffish, was practicing pliés in front of the mirror. She acted uninterested, but Maryellen saw her sneak peeks at what was happening by looking at the reflection in the mirror. Joan had lent Maryellen her round suitcase, which made her feel chic and sophisticated. She had to laugh when she found a soggy stuffed bear hidden in the suitcase under her pajamas. The bear was so wet, chewed, and bedraggled that she knew it had to be a joint contribution from Mikey and Scooter.

Mom came in with a box tied all around with string. "I thought that Grandmom might not have the energy to bake a Christmas coffee cake this year, what with taking care of Grandpop and all, so I made an extra one for you to bring," said Mom. "Ask Grandmom please to open the box right away, so the cake won't get stale. I packed things around it to protect it on the trip, but don't sit on it or let it get crushed, okay?"

"Okay," said Maryellen.

"Now, Ellie honey, you know that your grandmom and grandpop are elderly," Mom went on, sounding serious. "They have to take it easy, especially since Grandpop's been ill. So! Don't be rambunctious. And don't expect too much excitement."

"I understand, Mom," said Maryellen. "I'll be careful."

"Good," said Mom. She gave Maryellen a hug. "I know that I can trust you to be a considerate guest."

Maryellen didn't tell Mom that, in fact, she was rather looking forward to a quieter Christmas. In movies and on TV, Christmas morning wasn't messy and chaotic the way it was at the Larkins' house. Their family had a rule that no one could go into the living room until everyone was gathered. When Joan, who always groaned about how it was too early, finally agreed to get up, there was a stampede. With ten people opening presents, the living room was soon a sea of wrapping paper. One year, Tom stepped on a new doll Maryellen had just been given and broke its leg off and Scooter trotted off with the leg and buried it in the backyard, so that was the end of *that*. But at Grandmom and Grandpop's, Maryellen would be the only child. There would be no tussles over whose turn it was to open a present, or who had the biggest piece of coffee cake. There'd be no bossy Beverly queening it over everyone and telling them what to do. All would be calm, all would be *right*.

✳

The train station was crowded and bustling with holiday travelers. Everyone was happy and excited and in a hurry to begin his or her journey. Joan held Mikey, who hid his face in her neck because he was overcome by the commotion. Beverly was wide-eyed and subdued, and not at all her usual imperious, imperial self. Even Mom and Dad looked unusually intent.

Maryellen felt partly nervous and partly excited, which made her stomach fluttery. But she stood straight and tall, proudly holding her suitcase in one hand and the coffee-cake box in the other, as Mom gave her ticket to the porter and explained that Maryellen was traveling alone. The porter said that he'd keep an eye on her, and make sure that she got off the train in Atlanta.

"All aboard!" thundered a voice so loud, it seemed to fill the station.

Suddenly, it was time to say good-bye. Everyone hugged Maryellen, all talking at once. "When you come back, I want you to tell us what 'the moon on the breast of the new-fallen snow' looks like," said Dad with a wink.

"I will," Maryellen promised. Now her voice was fluttery, too.

Mom hugged Maryellen hard. "Give my love to Grandmom and Grandpop," she said. "Tell them I miss them terribly, and I wish I could see them. And remember, don't tire them out."

"I won't," said Maryellen. "Bye!" She spoke quickly, eager to be off before her nervousness won out over her excitement and her courage failed her. She turned and followed the porter up the steps of the train.

Maryellen was wearing her rain boots because they were too big to fit in her suitcase, so she kind of galumphed down the narrow corridor behind the porter. When he opened the door to her roomette, she gasped, "Oh, it's perfect!" There was a sweet little sink with a mirror over it and two comfortable plush seats facing each other next to the big square window that framed the view outside. She put her suitcase and the coffee-cake box under one seat. Then, remembering Karen King's advice, she sat on the seat facing forward and looked out the window. Her heart lurched just as the train lurched ahead and started to move, because there was her family lined up on the platform. They were all waving good-bye, except Beverly, who did *not* have the pom-pom hat on her head for a change. She had evidently also changed her mind about helping Maryellen, because she was doing an arabesque and pointing to her lifted chin.

"Good-bye," Maryellen called out, though she knew her family couldn't hear her. She waved until she couldn't see them anymore. The train left the station behind, chugging along faster and faster. Maryellen felt shivery with excitement. *Now!* she thought. *This is it. I'm beginning my adventure, all on my own!*

Maryellen took off her rain boots and put them under the seat next to her suitcase. Then, just because the little sink was so irresistible, she washed her hands. She wished her friends could see her, using the tiny bar of soap and the starched linen towel as casually as if she were a grown-up lady who traveled by herself every day. She smoothed her hair and then set forth for the observation car, which was the last car on the train. The observation car was set up like a long, nar-row living room, with chairs and tables and lamps. It had a dome roof made of glass and huge windows on both sides. Maryellen perched on a chair and watched the very last rays of the sun as it set over the Florida landscape. The sky turned orange, then it was purple streaked with pink, and finally it was a velvety black sprinkled with stars and pinned with a slender silvery sliver of moon.

In a short while, a porter walked through the observation car hitting a gong with a soft mallet. "Dinner is served," he said.

Maryellen followed him to the dining car and was given a seat at a table with a nice man and woman who had a little girl the same age as Mikey. The table had a crisp linen tablecloth on it, heavy china, shiny silver, and a little bouquet of flowers next to a small lamp. It was so elegant that Maryellen felt intimidated and self-conscious at first. But the little girl turned out to be just as messy an eater as Mikey, so Maryellen felt right at home as she ate her dinner of chicken noodle soup, meat loaf, mashed potatoes and peas, and pound cake for dessert.

"Are you traveling all by yourself?" asked the mother.

"Yes, ma'am," said Maryellen.

"My word!" said the mother.

"Now that's what I call plucky!" said the father.

Maryellen blushed and beamed.

After dinner, Maryellen went back to her roomette. While she had been gone, the porter had magically transformed the two seats into a bed. She put on her pajamas, washed at the little sink, and got into the bed. She propped herself up on her pillows, so that she could look out the window at the stars. *We're on our way, we're on our way,* the train seemed to be repeating, as if it were as excited as she was as it sped along, rocking Maryellen to sleep in her cozy, starry bed.

The Skaters' Waltz

✱ CHAPTER THIRTEEN ✱

T he next morning, it was still dark when the porter woke Maryellen. "Next stop, Atlanta," he said.

"Thanks," said Maryellen. She felt sort of groggy as she dressed and repacked her pajamas in her suitcase. But the minute she climbed down the steps off the train and onto the station platform, her grogginess fell away. The air was cold! It was so cool and clear and fresh that it cleared her head, too.

"Here she is, Mother!" Maryellen heard Grandpop say. And the next thing she knew, she was swept up into Grandpop's big arms, and Grandmom was smiling at her over his shoulder. "Cold enough for you, honey?" Grandpop asked.

"Yes!" said Maryellen joyfully.

"Come on along, then," said Grandpop. "We'll be

home in two shakes of a lamb's tail." He grinned as he tossed her suitcase into his old truck. "'Over the river and through the woods to your grandparents' house we'll go,'" he said in a singsong voice. "We don't have a horse-drawn sleigh, but you can roll down the window of the truck and stick your head out and pretend. How'll that be?"

"Great!" laughed Maryellen. She climbed into the truck and sat in the front, comfortably wedged between Grandmom and the door. At first, she didn't see any snow. But as Grandpop drove north out of Atlanta, the road began to weave its way up and down but mostly up, and soon the ground had a topping of snow as thin and fine and graceful as a spider's web.

"Oh, *look*!" cried Maryellen. "Snow! The first snow I've ever seen in real life!" It was just as enchanting as she had imagined it would be. The higher they drove, the more snow lay on the ground. The sun glinted off the snow that frosted rooftops and tree limbs. Under the trees, in the shadows, the snow was tinted blue. She took a deep breath. "Gosh," she said. "The snow even *smells* cold!"

"By gum, you're right!" said Grandpop.

The old truck creaked and clanked and jingled as they jounced along the mountain road, so it was very easy for Maryellen to imagine that she was in a sleigh with jingle bells.

She noticed that the colors here in the mountains were not the bright, tropical colors of Florida. They were muted and soft, so that when there was bright color, like the red of the holly berries or the quick flash of a cardinal, the red really stood out against the dusky background. Maryellen liked the way the leafless trees looked. The tall ones were bare black lines against the sky, some squiggly and some straight. They reminded her of her own doodles. The truck passed an apple orchard, and she saw that the weight of the snow had bent the branches so that they touched the ground, and the trees looked like ladies in lacy, hoopskirted dresses curtsying low to her as she rode past them.

As soon as Grandpop pulled into the driveway and stopped the truck, Maryellen hopped out and scooped up a handful of snow. First, she ate some. The snow tasted delicious and cold and just the tiniest bit piney, she decided. Then she made a snowball, packing the handful of snow into a smooth ball with her bare hands.

"Watch out!" teased Grandpop as he swung Maryellen's baggage out of the truck. "A snowball's as cold as a hot potato's hot!"

Maryellen grinned as she tossed the snowball into a snowbank. She was glad to see that Grandpop was as spry and jokey as ever. He certainly didn't *act* sick.

"Grandmom, is Grandpop over his sickness?" Maryellen asked as they went inside. The house smelled like cinnamon, and every window had a small holly wreath with a berry-red bow.

"Your Grandpop began to perk up the minute we got your letter," said Grandmom, smiling. Her dark eyes were as bright and shiny as a bird's. "And now that you're here, he's even perkier. You're a tonic for him, the old scalawag!"

"Scalawag?" repeated Grandpop as he came in with Maryellen's suitcase and box. "That must be me."

Maryellen laughed as she took the box from Grandpop and handed it to Grandmom. "Mom sent this Christmas coffee cake for you. She said to tell you that she misses you terribly and she wishes she could see you."

Grandmom looked a little sad and sorry as she took the coffee cake. "I wish I could see her, too," she said.

"This is the first Christmas we've ever spent apart."
Then Grandmom smiled at Maryellen. "It certainly
would have been a gloomy Christmas if you had not
come to cheer us up."

Grandmom asked Maryellen to set the table in
front of the fireplace for lunch. Maryellen looked at the
chimney and smiled at the thought of how reassuring
it would be to Beverly, Tom, and Mikey as a way for
Santa to enter the house.

She had just finished her lunch when Grandmom
tapped her on the hand and tilted her head toward the
window, saying, "Look!"

"It's snowing!" breathed Maryellen. There was
already a fresh little cap of snow on the bird feeder,
and a little black-and-white bird was pecking at the
birdseed.

"Better bundle up and go outside so's you can enjoy
it," said Grandpop. "I've never met a child yet who
didn't like to run around in a snowfall."

Maryellen pulled on her rain boots, her jacket, and
the scarf that Joan had given her and rushed outside.
She stood on the snow-covered lawn, held her arms
open wide, and tilted her head back so that the

snowflakes landed on her face. They were light and wet and cold and almost ticklish. Slowly, then faster and faster, she spun around, spinning herself dizzy in the swirling snow.

"So!" said Grandpop, joining her. "Is falling snow as pretty as you thought it would be?"

"No, it's prettier!" said Maryellen happily. "It's way better than on TV, because you can *feel* it."

"Come on, then," said Grandpop. He had an ax in one hand and pulled a sled with the other. "Let's go find that real pine Christmas tree you wrote about in your letter. I'll carry the ax. You pull the sled."

"Okay!" said Maryellen gaily.

She followed Grandpop up a narrow trail that twisted its way between fragrant pine trees. Snow sifted down through the branches and dusted the pine-needle-covered ground, making a soft carpet beneath her feet.

She carefully examined every tree that Grandpop pointed out to her. She considered nearly ten trees before she saw one that was just the right height and had just the right amount of bushiness. She took a deep breath. Ah! The tree smelled just right, too. It had the sharp, nose-tingly pine scent that she longed for.

"This is it," she said to Grandpop. "This is the per-fect tree."

Grandpop cut the tree down with a few strokes of his ax, and Maryellen helped him put it on the sled.

"Mom said she always wished that you could leave the tree outside because the snow was the prettiest decoration of all," Maryellen told Grandpop as they pulled the sled down the hill to the house.

"Well, I wish she could see *this* tree," said Grandpop. "By gum, I think it's the finest tree we've ever had. You're a good tree spotter, Miss Maryellen Larkin."

They left the tree on the porch to dry off a bit and stomped their feet hard to make the snow fall off their boots.

"Come in and sit next to the fire to warm up," said Grandmom. "Have some cocoa."

Maryellen was surprised to see a battered brown box tied with string on the floor in front of the fireplace.

"Open it up!" said Grandpop, his eyes twinkling. "It's not a Christmas present. It's just some things that used to belong to your mother. We thought they might come in handy for you today."

Maryellen untied the string and lifted the lid. "Oh!" she gasped. There was a short, red wool skating skirt and under it, beautiful powder-blue ice skates with sharp, shiny silver blades.

"I sharpened them and polished them up for you," said Grandpop. "They're good as new."

Maryellen hugged the skirt and the skates to her chest. She loved them because they were just like the jewelry-box skater's. "Oh, thank you!" she said. "They're perfect!"

"Well, put that skirt on and let's get this skating show on the road!" said Grandpop merrily, just as excited as Maryellen. "Winter afternoons are short, and the sun will soon be sinking behind the mountain."

Maryellen hurried to her room to change, and Grandmom came along to help her. Grandmom said it was so cold that she had to wear her pants under Mom's red skating skirt, so the skirt was a little snug around the waist. The skates looked a bit big, so Grandmom lent her some thick knitted socks to help them fit better. Maryellen tied Joan's scarf around her neck and hurried out to join Grandpop in the truck.

They were just about to pull away when Grandmom came rushing out of the house, waving something over her head. "Look what I found in the box with the coffee cake!" she said.

Maryellen recognized the mothball-y smell even before she saw what Grandmom was handing her. It was Beverly's stocking cap. Pinned to the pom-pom was a note in Beverly's printing that said: *Chin up.*

Maryellen had to grin as she pulled the hat onto her head. Beverly never missed a chance to be bossy!

Maryellen was quiet, tense, and eager as Grandpop drove the truck along a winding road that dipped and curved and wound around and up the mountain. The trees on either side of the road were so tall that they met overhead, so the road was like a secret tunnel. Grandpop turned onto a little side road that was hardly wider than a path, and . . .

"Ta-da!" said Grandpop. "There she is. There's your pond, Ellie-girl! I swept it clear yesterday, so there's only a little snow on it."

"Ahh," sighed Maryellen, enchanted.

The pond was just what Maryellen had imagined.

✳ The Skaters' Waltz ✳

It was secret, silent, and small. Pine trees crusted with snow ringed it all around, and now, because the sun was sinking, the snow was tinted pink. As she walked to the edge, she could see leaves suspended in the ice, frozen in place. She thought she might burst with happiness.

"Skate away!" said Grandpop. "Take all the time you want."

Maryellen tugged off her boots, tugged on the thick socks, laced on Mom's hand-me-down skates, and stepped gingerly onto the ice. At first, she was pretty shaky. It was a lot harder to balance on the ice skates' narrow blades than on the roller skates' four wheels. But she heard Beverly's voice in her head saying, "Chin up! Tummy in! Shoulders down!" She hummed "The Skaters' Waltz" softly to herself as she imagined Carolyn's plinking and plonking the tune on the piano. And pretty soon, she was skating—a little wobbly, but definitely skating! Joan's scarf fluttered out behind her, and Mom's old skating skirt fluttered, too. The pom-pom on Beverly's hat bounced gently on her back. Slowly, Maryellen leaned forward on one leg, lifted the other leg behind her, stretched her arms, and curved her hands just so in her arabesque, just as Beverly had shown her over and over again.

I'm doing it, thought Maryellen. *I'm the jewelry-box skater. I've made all my Christmas wishes come true.*

Maryellen knew that all the rest of her life, she'd never forget this moment. It was perfect, and yet . . . She suddenly found herself wishing her family could see her.

She closed her eyes, imagining that she was back in the carport on roller skates, with Beverly badgering her in French, Carolyn banging away on the piano, Tom and Mikey clapping, Joan correcting her clothes, and Scooter snoozing in the shade. It was the oddest thing! Here she was skating on the pond, in the snowy, serene scene she had yearned for, *ached* for, worked for, and all she could think of was how much she missed her family. And the biggest surprise of all was that the person she missed most was Beverly—persnickety, infuriating Queen Beverly. Only now did she realize how generous her little sister had been. Beverly had worked as hard as Maryellen to make her skating wish come true.

Maryellen skated until her ankles were aching, her knees numb, her fingers nearly frostbitten, her nose frozen, and her toes as cold as ten ice cubes, and then she skated some more. Despite the cold, she could tell that her skating was getting better and better. *Beverly would be pleased*, she thought. But inside, she was feeling worse and worse. Her heart felt heavy, and tears pricked her eyes. She knew they weren't just from the cold.

Because as she skated in that lovely silence, Maryellen began to see that she had made a terrible mistake. Somehow, she had been sort of bamboozled into thinking that Christmas had to do with how things *looked*. All the TV commercials and store windows and magazine ads and Christmas cards had tricked her. Suddenly she knew with absolute certainty that it wasn't how Christmas *looked* that was important. What mattered was how it *felt*. And it only felt right, she now realized, if you were surrounded by the people you loved most in the world.

As the sun slipped down below the treetops, Grandpop waved from the top of the bank. Maryellen waved back and skated over to the edge of the pond. She put on her boots, slung Mom's skates over her shoulder, trudged up the bank, and climbed into the truck. Her heart was as sore as her feet.

✴

The forlorn feeling grew stronger and stronger all evening. After dinner, she helped Grandmom and Grandpop bring the tree inside, and they decorated it with strings of popcorn and cranberries, felt birds, little red velvet bows, and painted pinecones. One last melting snowflake caught the light like a prism and sparkled like the diamond on a ring. *This would be the perfect tree for Joan and Jerry to get engaged by,* thought Maryellen, *but they're hundreds of miles away!* Every ornament made the tree more beautiful, and the more beautiful the tree became, the more she wished that her family could see the tree, too, and the more desperately she missed them.

✴

"Good night, sweetheart," Grandmom said softly as she tucked her into bed. Maryellen felt very strange to be in a room all by herself. It was so *quiet.* At home, in the room that she shared with Beverly, Carolyn, and Joan, someone was always tossing and turning.

Sometimes Scooter sneaked in and slept there too, and he snored. She had imagined that being an only child would be nice for a change. Instead, it felt lonely.

Grandmom went on, "My, but it is heavenly to have a little girl in the house at Christmastime again. Your Grandpop and I *still* miss having your mother here. We're sorry she lives so far away, especially at Christmas."

Maryellen hugged Grandmom close. She swallowed hard, trying not to cry, but one big sob escaped.

Grandmom pulled back and looked at Maryellen. She didn't even have to ask what was wrong. "You miss your family, don't you, honey?" she asked in her gentle way.

Maryellen nodded. Then she tried to explain. "The snow and the tree and skating on the pond were all more wonderful than I had imagined they'd be," she said. "And somehow, it's *because* they were so perfect, I realized that's not what makes Christmas *Christmas*."

Grandmom sighed. She didn't say anything. She just pulled Maryellen close.

"What's the matter, Mother?" asked Grandpop, hovering worriedly in the doorway. "Is the child sick?"

"Mm-hmm," said Grandmom. "Homesick."

"There's only one cure for that!" Grandpop said mysteriously. "And I've got it. We'll just have to take Ellie home."

Maryellen sat bolt upright in bed. *"What?"* she and Grandmom both asked at once.

"I've been thinking about this all day!" said Grandpop. He was so excited that he almost reminded Maryellen of herself when she got carried away by one of her big ideas. "We can put the Christmas tree in the truck. The ornaments aren't breakable, so they'll be fine. We'll drive through the night. We'll miss the sunrise church service on the pier, but we'll be in Daytona Beach bright and early Christmas morning."

"But," Maryellen sputtered, "I thought you didn't feel well enough to make that trip."

"So did I!" laughed Grandpop. "So did I! I thought my get-up-and-go had got up and went. But you've done me a world of good, Ellie-girl. You've livened me up no end. I'm not such an old geezer as I thought— not yet anyway." He turned to Grandmom and asked, "What do you say, Mother? Are you game?"

Grandmom's face glowed. "I'll make a thermos of

coffee and pack some sandwiches," she said. "If we put snow in the cooler, they'll stay fresh all the way—and Ellie can bring her brothers and sisters some snow for Christmas!"

Maryellen's heart soared with hope, but she felt worried, too. "I've already caused you so much extra work and trouble," she said. "I can't ask you to do *this*, too."

"Hogwash," said Grandpop. "You *didn't* ask. It was *my* idea! And I think it's a corker."

"I do, too," said Grandmom. She smiled at Maryellen. "All's I know is, you and your 'extra trouble' made *my* Christmas wishes come true. I wanted Grandpop to feel better, and I wanted to be with your family. Thanks to you, to my surprise, it looks like I'm going to get both of my wishes."

"I'm going to go put the tree in the truck," said Grandpop. "Shake a tail feather, ladies. Santa's sleigh will be leaving soon!" Grandpop left singing, "Over the river and through the woods to Daytona Beach we'll go!"

In a jiffy, Maryellen found herself bundled into blankets and settled cozily like a bird in a nest between

Grandpop and Grandmom in the truck. She took one long, last look at the snow so that she could describe how it looked with the moon shining on it, as she had promised Dad she would. The moon was too slender to give the snow "the luster of mid-day," but she thought its soft lavender glow was beautiful.

Grandpop handed Maryellen a map. "You can be my navigator," he said. "Just get me to Route 1, and then you can fall asleep. Route 1 will take us right into Daytona Beach."

Maryellen actually stayed awake until after they crossed the border into Florida and were headed to Jacksonville. By then, her head felt as heavy as a stone, and she fell asleep on Grandmom's soft shoulder.

✳

The warmth and light of the rising sun woke her up. Her senses told her that she was home before she even opened her eyes. She could feel the sun on her face, and smell the scent of the salty, sandy beach mixed with just a hint of citrusy orange in the balmy air.

Grandpop stopped the truck on the street in front of Maryellen's house, and they all climbed out, stretching their stiff legs. "Well, ladies," Grandpop said as he lifted the pine tree out of the truck. "We're here. You ring the doorbell, Ellie."

Maryellen ran up the front walk and pushed the doorbell. *Ding-dong.* Then she opened the front door, and she and Grandmom and Grandpop stepped inside, calling out, "Surprise!"

As everyone stampeded toward them, exclaiming and laughing with delight, Grandpop said, "I've got a special delivery here for the Larkin family. It's a great little girl named Ellie. And a Christmas tree, too!"

And then, what a commotion! Dad swept Maryellen off her feet. Mom hugged Grandmom, and they both cried a little bit, but Maryellen knew they were tears of happiness. Mikey flung his arms around Grandpop's legs and held on for dear life. Beverly and Tom cheered and clapped and jumped up and down, chanting, "Ellie! Grandmom! Grandpop!" Scooter barked with gusto. Carolyn banged out something that sounded pretty close to "Joy to the World" on the piano, and Joan just kept saying, "I can't believe it! I can't *believe* it!"

Grandpop, sounding very pleased with himself, was crowing, "We surprised you this time, didn't we? You should see your faces! By golly! We sure did surprise *you*."

"I've never been so astonished in my life!" said Mom. "How on earth did you decide to drive all this way?"

"Well, Ellie gets the credit," said Grandpop. "She made us see that the presents we wanted most was your *presence*! So I said to Mother, 'Come on, Mother, old girl! We're not so old that we can't spring a surprise on the kids, now, are we? Let's take Ellie-girl home for Christmas.' And here we are!"

"Oh, I am so *glad*," said Dad, hugging Maryellen close.

"We haven't even opened our presents yet!" said Carolyn.

Mom turned to Maryellen. "Didn't you like your Christmas in the mountains?" she asked.

"Oh, I did!" said Maryellen. "It was wonderful! It snowed, and Grandpop and I went into the woods to find the perfect Christmas tree. Then I skated on a pond, and it was just as magical as I had imagined it would be. But—but I missed everybody here so much. It just didn't feel right without you."

Mom smiled. "It didn't feel right without you, either," she said. "Thank goodness you're all here."

"Well, now that everybody's all together, let's have Christmas!" said Dad.

He and Grandpop stood the evergreen tree in an empty wastebasket and wedged it upright with bricks. Then they put it in front of the bookcases, next to the pink tree. It tilted a bit and the ornaments were askew, but no one cared. The tree's piney scent filled the room and, it seemed to Maryellen, brought with it the fresh coolness of the mountains.

They had just begun to hand out presents when the doorbell rang. Scooter barked and howled, *"Ar-ooo! Ar-ooo!"*

"Who on earth could *that* be?" asked Mom over the ruckus.

"At this point, I wouldn't be surprised to see President Eisenhower—or Santa himself," said Dad as he went to open the door.

There stood Jerry. "Merry Christmas, everyone!" he said. Then he walked straight over to Joan, who was sitting on the floor next to the pink plastic Christmas tree sharing a piece of coffee cake with Mikey. "I love you,

Joan," said Jerry. "Will you marry me?"

Joan's mouth was full, so she nodded as she chewed, swallowed, and said, "Okay!" Then she jumped up and hugged Jerry as everyone clapped and cheered. Dad thumped Jerry on the back, Grandpop shook his hand, and Mom and Grandmom hugged Joan. It was the least romantic proposal Maryellen had ever seen; it was not at all the way people got engaged at Christmastime in the movies. There was no candlelight or music, Joan was in her pajamas with her hair in pin curls, the entire family plus Scooter was watching, and Jerry didn't even have a ring. But by now, Maryellen knew that how something *looked* didn't matter at all. What mattered was how it *felt*, and she knew that Jerry's proposal—and Joan's answer—came straight from the heart. Maryellen was so glad she had not missed it.

It was a long time before everyone settled down enough to go back to the important business of opening gifts. Mom handed Maryellen a wrapped present. "Merry Christmas, sweetie," she said.

When Maryellen unwrapped the present, she smiled. It was the jewelry box. Gently, she lifted the lid. The little skater twirled on her tiny foot, spinning around and around on the mirror pond to the tune of "The Skaters' Waltz." "Oh, Mom, thank you!" said Maryellen.

In a quiet voice Beverly asked, "Is that what it was like when you were skating, Ellie?"

"Yes," said Maryellen. She smiled at Beverly. "Thank you for teaching me. You worked so hard to help me make my wish come true. I couldn't have done it without you." Maryellen handed Beverly the present she had made for her. "I think you really deserve this."

Beverly unwrapped it. "A crown!" she exclaimed. Immediately, Beverly put the crown on her head. She rose up on her toes, lifted her arms above her head, and spun around while everyone—especially Maryellen— applauded loudly for her.

When it was quiet, Maryellen lifted the lid of her jewelry box so that the music played and the little skater twirled on the mirror. As she imagined her-self back on the pond in the snowy, piney woods, she knew with all the certainty of her heart that the true magic of Christmas was right here, at home, with her noisy family around her. She turned the jewelry box so that everybody could see the little skater. "I loved my snowy, old-fashioned Christmas," she said. "It was beautiful and lovely and perfect. It just wasn't a *real* Christmas without all of you."

INSIDE Maryellen's World

The 1950s were years of peace, prosperity, promise, and exuberant growth in the United States. World War Two was over, and the economy was booming. Families were booming, too, and big families like Maryellen's were not unusual. In fact, so many children were born during this era that it became known as the "Baby Boom." Jobs were plentiful as industries switched from making wartime products to making goods for families to buy. Homeowners like the Larkins were proud of their new appliances and modern conveniences. Neighbors would often gather to admire big new purchases such as cars and televisions!

In Maryellen's time, television shows were in black and white, and networks broadcast only a few hours each day. Whole families would gather to watch popular comedies such as *I Love Lucy,* Westerns such as *The Lone Ranger,* and variety shows such as *The Ed Sullivan Show.* Only a few channels were available, so most people watched the same news shows, programs, and advertisements. This gave newscasters and advertisers great power to shape the public's view of life, yet TV didn't always depict life accurately. For example, women were usually shown as housewives even though millions of women worked outside the home. And except for a few Indians in Westerns, almost everyone on TV was white. Americans whose lives didn't match the television version of life sometimes felt out of step—the way Maryellen felt about Christmas in sunny, sandy Florida.

Advertisers and manufacturers encouraged Americans to "keep up with the Joneses" by having cars, furniture, and appliances that were as nice as their neighbors', so that people would buy lots of new goods. Even the government encouraged *conformity*, or agreement and sameness. Although the United States was not officially at war with the Soviet Union, the two countries were deeply suspicious of each other and had a hostile relationship known as the *Cold War*. People who were suspected of friendly feelings toward the Soviet Union could be *black-listed*, which meant they might be fired from their jobs and questioned by the government. When this happened, sometimes their former friends treated them badly, too. Maryellen feels this pressure to conform when she makes friends with Angela, the Italian girl.

But many Americans look back on the 1950s as fun and happy years full of optimism. Middle-class children like Maryellen had comfortable lives, with more opportunities for education and entertainment than any previous generation of children. TV encouraged conformity, but it also broadened people's views by showing how other people lived and bringing the whole world right into peoples' living rooms. Just like Maryellen, many Americans felt energized, inspired, and challenged to find a balance between being what people wanted or expected them to be and being unique or "one and only."

Read more of MARYELLEN'S stories,
available from booksellers and at *americangirl.com*

✳ *Classics* ✳
Maryellen's classic series, now in two volumes:

Volume 1:
The One and Only
Maryellen wants to stand out—
but when she draws a cartoon
of her teacher, she also draws
unwanted attention. Still, her
drawing skills help her make a
new friend—with a girl her old
friends think of as an enemy!

Volume 2:
Taking Off
Maryellen's birthday party is a
huge hit! Excited by her fame,
she enters a science contest. But
can Maryellen invent a flying
machine *and* get her sister's
wedding off the ground?

✳ *Journey in Time* ✳
Travel back in time—and spend a day with Maryellen!

The Sky's the Limit
Step into Maryellen's world of the 1950s! Go to a sock hop, or take
a road trip with the Larkin family all the way to Washington, D.C.
Choose your own path through this multiple-ending story.

✳ A Sneak Peek at ✳

Taking Off

A Maryellen Classic
Volume 2

Maryellen's adventures continue in the
second volume of her classic stories.

ahoo!" shrieked Maryellen.

To celebrate the last day of school, Mom had cut up a chilled watermelon and set up the oscillating sprinkler in the front yard. Within minutes of being home from school, Maryellen and Beverly were in their bathing suits running through the deliciously cold sprinkler water. Scooter, lying with his jaw on his paws, watched from the shade.

Suddenly Beverly said, with wide eyes, "Look!"

Dad was turning into their driveway, and attached to his car was a huge silver trailer. Dad honked the car horn, and Mom, Joan, and Carolyn came dashing out of the house.

"What on earth is that?" asked Mom when everyone had settled down a bit.

"Isn't it a beauty?" said Dad, patting the trailer proudly. "It's the 1955 Airstream. And it's all ours. We are going to see the U.S.A. this summer, kids, and this will be our home away from home."

"Can we go inside it?" Maryellen asked.

"Sure!" said Dad.

Inside, the Airstream was shipshape and trim. Maryellen had never seen anything so fabulously modern but also comfortable and homey. The kitchen was in the middle, just across from the door. There was a tiny sink, refrigerator, stove, and shelves.

"Look how darling the kitchen is!" cooed Carolyn. "It has everything a regular kitchen has, only miniature."

"Get a load of this, honey," Dad said to Mom. He opened a cupboard and pulled down an ironing board.

"I'm thrilled," said Mom, though she didn't sound as though she really was.

To the left of the kitchen were a bed and a closet, and the whole back end was a bathroom. Maryellen poked her head in. "There's even a bathtub and shower!" she exclaimed.

Finally, the excitement quieted down and Mom called the family to dinner. Everyone went inside reluctantly. The house seemed awfully sprawling and dull, compared with the sleek and snazzy Airstream.

Mom plunked a tuna-noodle casserole onto the table and then sat down and sighed.

"What's the matter, dear?" Dad asked.

"Well," said Mom, "I just wish that you had consulted me before you bought such a—well, such a whopping huge purchase."

"I wanted it to be a surprise," said Dad.

"It's a surprise, all right," said Mom. "I never

expected to have a gigantic silver rocket ship parked in our driveway."

"Oh, it won't be parked in our driveway for long," said Dad. "This summer, we're taking a family road trip."

"A road trip?" asked Mom. "You mean we won't be going to visit my parents?" Every summer before this, the Larkins had gone to the Georgia mountains to stay with Grandmom and Granpop for vacation.

"Well," said Dad. "I thought we'd head out West. It's high time the kids saw some of the wide-open spaces of the U.S.A. west of the Mississippi."

"I love the idea of heading west!" gushed Maryellen. Just about all of her favorite TV shows were Westerns. She pictured herself riding a galloping horse across the sagebrush prairie, sleeping out under the stars, and crossing raging rivers like the pioneers. "Please can we go to the Alamo, Dad?" she begged. "Davy Crockett was there."

"Don't expect the West to still look the way it does in those ridiculous Westerns that you watch on TV," cautioned Joan. "And Davy Crockett? I can't believe you idolize a guy who walked around with a dead raccoon on his head."

Mom held up both hands to stop the whole dis-
cussion. She looked harried. "I've got Joan and Jerry's
wedding breathing down my neck," she said to Dad.
"There's still so much to do. The painters are coming next week to get the house ready for the wedding.
Who'll supervise them—Scooter?"

"Scooter will come with us," said Dad, "And wouldn't
you like a vacation from all the wedding worries?"

"Mom," said Maryellen, "what if Grandmom and
Granpop came here? That way, we could see them, and
they could take care of the house while we're gone and
be sure the painters are doing everything right. They
could stay for a while after our trip, too, so that we
could have a nice long visit together."

Mom considered her suggestion. "That might
work," she said, nodding and smiling a little.

"That's a great idea, Ellie," said Dad, beaming.

Maryellen turned eagerly to Mom. "I'll take care of
Scooter on the trip, I promise." Truthfully, she didn't
think that being responsible for lazy, sleepy Scooter
would be very hard. She added, "I'll help with other
chores, too."

"All right," said Mom. She shrugged in surrender.
"Westward ho, I guess."

About the Author

VALERIE TRIPP says that she became a writer because of the kind of person she is. She says she's curious, and writing requires you to be interested in everything. Talking is her favorite sport, and writing is a way of talking on paper. She's a daydreamer, which helps her come up with her ideas. And she loves words. She even loves the struggle to come up with just the right words as she writes and rewrites. Ms. Tripp lives in Maryland with her husband.